FROM INTERNATIONAL BESTSELLING AUTHOR
KIA CARRINGTON-RUSSELL

MAD HATTER VAMPIRE PRINCE

CRYSTAL
PUBLISHING

MAD HATTER VAMPIRE PRINCE
Copyright © 2020 by Kia Carrington-Russell

ISBN: 978-0-6484981-6-2 (Kindle)
ISBN: 978-0-6484981-7-9 (Paperback)

CRYSTAL
◆ PUBLISHING ◆

THE MAD HATTER VAMPIRE PRINCE

A *wicked Vampire Novella*
A prequel based on the Token Huntress series.

By Kia Carrington-Russell

DEDICATION

Thank you to those who are always in my corner
encouraging me to do what I love and to live my life free as a bird.
You know who you are, and you all inspire me for different reasons.
Thank you to the friends that I made during my time in Scotland
where I wrote this book.
Adventures, laughs and dreams- always.

They called him a clown, who had a crown, and who would never look down on his left.

For the people were less, and humanity was far from blessed, and would only act as his entertainment.

He would fixate on some, and bathe in the blood of the rest, for he had been known as a vampire.

Magnificent, treacherous, and flamboyant as could be.

But one day appeared, a tiny mouse beside his throne that made him look down to his right in curiosity.

She had a name, that he would soon learn—but perhaps it would already be too late.

CHAPTER
I

THE MAD HATTER VAMPIRE PRINCE

"How in God's name did I get raked into this boredom?" I snarled displeased. I sat on the oversized throne raking my pointed nails against its armchair. The marble room was bright with white tiles and polished as it always had been. The gold trimmings sparkled against the bold glass chandeliers that hung from the ceiling. I uncomfortably sat from side to side on the cushions that were far too used to my brother's mold instead.

"For the eighth time that I'm explaining it yet again; your brother had other affairs to attend to and as first prince, it is your responsibility to step in and listen to the people from time to time," Galador said in his dry and whimsical voice. I flopped myself back dramatically huffing, annoyed that I had somehow agreed. I looked up at the old vampire who looked no older than mid-thirties. He dressed like an outdated housewife with a spark of boring ass butler. I grumbled to myself. How had my company fallen so low? I could be entertaining myself in splendor, instead I was amusing this old bore. I twisted to look at him at a better angle.

"I wonder, Galador," I said, now having slight interest in him. "Did you change your hair recently?" Galador's blue eyes slowly and begrudgingly diverted from the large wooden doors at the end of the exaggerated and lengthy room and fell upon me. He had been serving my family, more specifically my father, and then brother, for hundreds of years. My brother had now been in ruling for seventy-five years. He stuck to the traditions and old ways of my father, which I found utterly primitive. In retrospect, I stayed away from the throne as much as possible because it seemed painfully boring. You had to ask for permission before killing anyone. We were vampires for fuck's sake! We should be able to fuck, kill, and trick whomever we wanted without thinking of the political maneuver behind it. If being on the top of the food chain and ruling over humans were results of this, I wish we just ate every last one. At least the only temptation of fun was the whisper of war amongst our own kind. It offered me hope because there were a few stray rebels and Kings who knew how to have some fun in this boring world.

Galador slid his hand over his sleek blonde hair that was never a strand out of place. "No, your majesty, I have not." No shit. Because you don't change ever. None of us do. "Now please focus, your first attendee is about to enter." I grumbled in response as with perfect timing, the large wooden doors at the end of the room opened wide. I stared past the man that strode in. Beyond his broken posture, the world outside this room was bright and glimmered of freedom. I could be out there, minding my own business and crafting my own entertainment.

We couldn't stand or persevere through natural sunlight. One of the downfalls of being a creature of the night. But with technological advances our throne and city had been one of few that crafted a dome over our Kingdom. We were able to produce artificial day and night that we could walk amongst without combusting and lumping into a decaying mass. We were no longer simply creatures of the night that could only stalk during the night but advanced to something more, something–

"Dear God, kill him! That attire is atrocious!" I screamed at the man that was walking towards me. Immediately he looked panicked. "Guards!" I shouted. They began to move from the sides of the walls on my demand. The overfed man became defensive. How boring, why did they always plea for their life? How I prayed for the day that a human would be less predictable and a little more exciting, if only slightly.

"Kyran!" Galador reprimanded me. "You're in the throne room. You can't so quickly choose to a kill a man because of what he is wearing."

"People have been killed for less crimes in the past," I said looking over my shoulder at him. The man was an eyesore. Galador was not impressed. I sighed. It would be so much more entertaining to see the fat man shake in his boots and possibly shit himself. But oh no, Galador was more censored to this leadership business than I was. I sighed again, not because my body needed breath but because I enjoyed its dramatic response. I was disappointed that he really wasn't going to let me have any fun during this torturous hour. I wavered my hand at the guards who proceeded to step back. Fine. Let the man live.

"Tha- Thank you, your majesty. I wasn't aware that it would be Prince Kyran I would be speaking with today," He stumbled over his words, still trying to regain his shallow breath. Icky human.

"If you had, would you have brought me a gift in hopes that I would say yes to whatever your overbearing request is?" I threw my legs over the armchair of the throne slumping in it trying to discover any comfortable angle on this tarnished chair. This was already taking far too long.

The man offered a timid smile and crumpled his paperwork slightly. Fuck, was he going to give me a presentation?

"Perhaps, so that I don't inconvenience you. I will come back next month to speak with King Amell?" The man tattered.

I clasped my hands in joy, the man jumped–frightened. One of my favorite expressions to see. "I think that would work out perfectly, have a nice day!" Without a second of delay the man walked back through the doors with a speed he didn't come in on.

"Kyran," Galador grumbled. "The point of this is so you can aid your brother, not to create a backlog of attendees next month for him."

"You're right... Should I just kill him?" With Galador's disapproving glare I knew the answer was no. "Such a buzzkill Galador, when was the last time you had fun?"

"Bring in the next one!" he shouted to permit the next to come through. I sighed, waiting for the young vampire to take his stride, he seemed far too confident. The little shit irritated me with his cocked swagger.

"I'm a huge fan," the vampire said with a smile, his little fangs gleaming with mischief. I smiled back, the impression not reaching my eyes.

"I'm quite the fan of myself as well," I said looking at my sharpened nails.

"I suppose that's something we will agree on today," he agreed with a snake's smile. Surprising; he hadn't lost his spirit. He began to babble on about needing more currency for his company's upcoming project. They needed support from the throne so they could hire more laborers. I looked between him and then Galador, entirely bored. How my brother sat through this, *seriously* baffled me.

"So, in short," I cut him off after hearing enough. "You want funds so you can speed up the building process. You've come to me with a proposal but what I'm understanding is that you want fancier shit and material for your design and projecting that it's all in the interest and benefit to your King. None of what you're telling me actually insinuates it's going to be built faster or that it will be beneficial to me."

"To the Kingdom," Galador corrected.

"Yeah, the Kingdom," I said wavering him off. I could feel the effective eyeroll behind me. "So, *son*, my word of advice is to work harder and stop holding out your hand for free shit. I've been advised that I can't kill anyone today, but can I chop off his hand?" I swiveled to ask Galador seriously. "Maybe just a few fingers?"

"Your proposal is rejected. You may leave," Galador said to the young vampire. I grumbled and slapped my face into my propped hand.

"Well perceived," Galador said. I rolled my eyes. It was as if he was praising me like a lecturer would their student. One of the guards reported to Galador that more than half of those who were waiting for an audience today had left. I couldn't prevent the smirk that so cunningly spread on my face.

Galador growled and I was so overjoyed that my reputation perceived me. Galador waved his hand, requesting the guards to open the doors yet again. I stared at the opening doors waiting for another pathetic lump to stride in. If it was worse than the previous two, I would undoubtedly find a sudden fixation on the expensive chandeliers. Maybe I would even study the paintings in the room that exemplified our family's history. Had my life become so boring that staring at antique paintings would be my only form of entertainment for the day?

A lightly armored human walked in. My eyebrows perked. Her hips swayed with little effort and bold confidence. Her golden hair was tied back tightly as her brown steely eyes fixed on me. She had two swords strapped to her back. Weapons weren't often allowed in this room. Which meant she was an exception—which concluded she was *interesting*.

The light clatter of her shoes echoed throughout the room. I sat upright now entirely intrigued by this beauty. My newfound composure was not missed by Galador who looked at the woman with increased interest. A waft of her natural scented perfume evaded my senses. A very feminine and floral scent mixed with a steely poison that rubbed raw against my nose. An interesting mix. I licked over the points of my fangs, so badly wanting to see if the smell of her was identical to the taste of her blood. I was far too old to lose control from initial distraction. Though I often chose to act on what I wanted impulsively. Instead, I wanted to enjoy her aroma and sunk into a comfier composure in the throne. What fun little mouse had come into my kingdom today?

"I was under the impression that I'd be meeting with King Amell today," she said. Her voice was strong and unwavering despite being the only human in a roomful of vampires. Something about her stance told me she could hold her own too, despite the obvious disadvantage. Her sleeveless leather shirt revealed her toned muscles underneath. Arms that were built and strong enough to wield two swords at once. Her stance and harsh brown eyes told me everything I needed to know about her. She was a fighter. She was a warrior. And she was fierce.

"And instead the Gods have smiled upon you today and presented you before me," I said with a charming smile that had never failed.

"Can I have your word that you will take this seriously, or should I leave and wait for the King next month?" she asked abruptly. Although no one moved in the room, I could sense the uncomfortable stature of everyone. They were considering how I might react. No human ever had the audacity to speak to me in such a fine goading way. I let out a monstrous laugh. Oh, she would be fun.

"You do not speak to the Prince that way," Galador reprimanded, obviously irritated that I hadn't already done so myself. "Introduce yourself formally. Don't offend the throne any further."

I propped my elbow up and rested my face in the palm of my hand. I couldn't help but sweep my gaze up her legs. I had no doubt that her hidden legs were as muscular as the rest of fighting fit body. Her face though—her face was what drew me in so forcefully. She held such a stern expression that probably hadn't seen laughter for years. It was beautiful. Ruthless, calculated, and unforgiving. A large jagged scar ran down the right side of her neck. Either a vampire had tried to take her life most savagely or someone had cut her deep in a fight. I grasped hard on the armchair. Surprising even myself by how much that disturbed me. What an interesting pull to have towards such a woman, a human of all things. I was aroused by my sudden interest in such a tiny mouse.

Without apology, she introduced herself. "My name is Sasha Pierce. I'm here in my father's stead today, Captain Mile Pierce. We stand guard over your walls." I knew that the last added part was because she assumed, I had no idea who either of them were. *It might've been close to the truth.* Humans guarded our walls so we would never be exposed to the risk of real sunlight. They were the hounds at our doors. They were elite fighters who despite the difference in speed and strength, could hold their own in a fight with the weapons they crafted. They were lovely little guard dogs.

"And what does this little wall sitter want from me?" I patronized.

"I want nothing from you," she said bashfully. I couldn't contain my smile yet again, which did nothing to unsettle her. "I've come to ask the King, if he would allow us to start exhibitions outside of the wall."

"That's preposterous, we already have an elite team for that," Galador interrupted. I rose my finger to him and he immediately silenced. He was taken aback but didn't speak another word.

"Didn't you say that I was making the decisions today," I reprimanded him with a cocky grin. I turned to Sasha with a predatory gaze. I had a reputation befitting of me amongst the many Kingdoms of our land. Most either feared me or crazily obsessed over me. But this one was different, no signs of either. I jumped off my seat and with lightning speed, came to a halt to stand in front of her. A breeze swept past her from my speed, but no clothing or hair moved. It was all so tightly pinned back just like this woman. I circled her, assessing her more seriously at a closer advantage.

Her scent was driving me crazy. I stepped closer and pressed my nose to her neck and inhaled. The surprisingly floral and feminine smell flooded me and inevitably made me thirsty for her. But the pang of copper shortly came through with an undertone of grit to my pallet. My cock began to throb with anticipation. Strange that she hadn't so much as flinched since I approached her so closely. She just stood, frozen like a well-trained soldier. My cock throbbed for her as I circled once again. I brushed back part of her leather collar to see how far the scar stretched down her neck. I couldn't see the ending.

"Who did this to you?" I asked. I wanted to know who and how I could find them. It had been a while since I had ventured on a scavenger hunt.

"You don't intimidate me," was her response. I arched my eyebrows and stood in front of her. I was not oblivious to my own overpowering presence and physical appearance. Some had proclaimed me as a beautiful death angel. I hadn't met anyone yet that could so easily look into my crystal blue eyes and not become short of breath. I was glorified in my maddening reputation and looks. But not this woman. My own arrogance began to eat at me alive. I wanted the gratification of her attraction towards me.

"If not intimidation then do I thrill you in other ways?" I said in a husky tone that would make most whimper and plea. Again, her body gave me no indication of interest. She just matched my stare with those steely brown eyes. Was she... bored?

"Not in the slightest," she said. She looked over my shoulder and began to speak to Galador, ignoring me entirely. "There's been an increase of movement outside the walls during the day which indicates that they are human. If we had scouts further out, we could catch them and bring them back. Your elite vampire team cannot approach them outside the wall while the sun is up. They aren't enough."

"How dare you—" I cut Galador off with a monstrous cackle. I stepped in front of her sight yet again so that she couldn't see past my shoulders. Her gaze was relentless. I pressed my hand around her throat very slowly in consideration. She didn't react in anyway. *So controlled.* Had it been anyone else, I would've snapped their neck for ignoring me by now. I contemplated it. Her throat bobbled. She was only human. Slowly she slid her hand behind her back to reach for the handle of her sword. In those few seconds the soldiers that stood silently against the walls stepped forward. I couldn't help but chuckle. As if I needed such protection from one measly human at that. My brother had become too comfortable within his cushioned position if he was relying on his guards.

"Although I love the confidence little lamb," I purred. "You shouldn't overestimate your own ability and underestimate *me*. If I desired it, you would already be dead." I stroked over the jagged scar on her neck. My thumb trailed over it as I contemplated what I would do with this new toy of mine.

I removed my hand from her throat, no longer able to sustain the proximity. As soon as I touched and began stroking her scarred skin, I wanted to fuck her and claim her as mine. An oddity but tastefully interesting.

"I'll permit this to happen on two conditions," I said and walked back to the throne with deliberate slowness. I had my back to her. If she was stupid enough to attack me, she could do so now. I raised my finger to Galador who was about to oppose the matter.

"What are your conditions?" She asked. I smiled. She took the bait.

"One, you will be my personal bodyguard as of tomorrow until I trust you are equipped enough for such exhibitions."

"You don't seem to need a bodyguard, your majesty," she gritted out the last part. Oh my, now we were full of formalities.

"Call me Kyran, that's what my friends call me." I looked

up at the chandeliers and considered that. "Well, if I had friends. If you refuse, then I will outright deny your request."

She gritted her teeth and took a loud exhale. After a quick calculation she released her hand from the sword. "And your second condition?"

I charmed a smile and took a place in my seat once again. "I will join you on any exhibition I so desire. Only when it is at night of course."

"Your majesty," Galador exclaimed. "That is madness. Why–"

"No Galador, it sounds fun. I only go on exhibitions when brother wants me to kill villages of people at a time. There's been less requests lately and I'm bored." I offered him puppy dog eyes. Galador was taken aback. No one could ever change my mind once I had decided on something. And this was something fun and delicious. Delicious she would be. "Well what do you say little mouse?"

"That I feel like I am making a deal with the devil," she admitted. I snaked a smile. She wasn't an idiot and it excited me how weary yet confident she was within my presence.

"Does the devil look this good?" I asked raking my hand down my body.

"The devil doesn't talk so much," she said with a steely tone. I laughed again. Oh, my how fun her quip tongue would be. I could imagine how fun and great it would be at other things. My cock throbbed again. Fuck me, if she didn't leave the room soon, I would pounce on her before she reached the door.

"Then it's a deal Miss Pierce. I'll see you tomorrow. Dismissed," I waved her off, becoming uncomfortable with how much I wanted to dive into her and make her my own.

I held onto the armchairs to restrain myself from chasing after her to do exactly that. I licked over my fangs as she turned and walked out the doors. The taste of my own blood downed my throat as I watched her ass shift back and forth in her leather pants. This day didn't turn out so bad after all. I just found a very interesting mouse who might be able to play a very fun game with me.

CHAPTER
2

TEA PARTY

"THIS IS RIDICULOUS," SASHA SAID, sitting opposite to me. The male human beside me was giggling as I sprayed his wrist into my cup. He was cute and would make a rather nice snack later in the day for separate matters. I swirled the warm blood in my china cup.

"Oh, I'm sorry did you want one?" I asked offering her my glass. I stirred in a few herbs that I delighted in. She refused my offer. By how boldly she denied me it was evident she had never seen a fancy fucking tea before. "I accommodated twelve different types of herbal teas especially for you, you simply have to choose one."

I pointed to the table between us that had an assortment of biscuits and such to keep my human well fed. We sat in the botanic garden that was fluttering with butterflies and birds. I was certain there were even exotic animals such as tigers in here. It had been so many years since I had personal guests and used this space that I wasn't sure what lived in here anymore.

"I still don't understand why you had me taken from my position and guarding the wall to have a tea party with you," she seethed, and oh how she was angry.

"Sasha you seem like an angry person," I began as point of conversation. I set my blue china cup down and uncrossed my legs. "Maybe I can teach you to loosen up. I'm certain that eventually you will be so daring as to give me a smile."

She stared at me in disbelief. "Many of my men and women have died protecting your walls… so you can have tea parties. Forgive me that I don't see light-hearted humor in this meeting."

"You're forgiven." I shrugged my shoulders accepting her insincere apology. "So obviously no boyfriend then?" I asked, crossing my legs. Not that I cared if she did. It would make no difference to me. If looks could kill, I'd be dead. I let a coy smile out. How I delighted in that hatred. I picked up my tea, taking a mouthful of the coppery herbs. I was praying on the beating vein in her neck. I could be consuming the very creature sitting before me instead of entertaining her in this sophisticated stage that I never used. "Tell me Sasha, how do you see me?"

She responded without hesitation. "I think that you've gone crazy during the hundreds of years that you've lived. You lack in ambition and act as your brothers lap dog. I'm surprised very few have attempted to take your life and genuinely believe that your arrogance will be your undoing."

I furrowed my eyebrows in confusion. "No, no, I meant my looks. Are you attracted to me?" She looked at me dumbfounded and I charmed her another smile. "Play with me."

She looked away with a sigh that sounded imprisoned for eternity. I took a loud sip to draw her attention back to me. Tick tock. Tick tock. The mouse will come around the clock. She turned again and straightened her shoulders. Much to my shock she flashed her pearly whites with a smile that I thought I would never see.

"Well," she purred. "You look to be a man in his late twenties. You have pale, smooth, and beautiful skin. Well built in frame, muscular, six foot six in height. You have nice trimmed black hair with a little bit of shadow instead of a full-grown beard. You have a strong muscular jaw and pointed nose with bold dark eyebrows that so beautifully frame those piercing blue eyes that seem to look into my soul every time our eyes meet. You hold a daring confidence that lets any woman in the room know that you are no good for her." I prompted her to continue. This was the conversation I had been waiting for in the last twenty-four hours. She provided pause and I took that in with a smile. She was attracted to me. "Such a beautiful man, such an intoxicating vampire. And yet," the charming smile she held vanished. "I find myself utterly repulsed."

I slowly put my tea down not letting my gaze drop from hers. "Are you certain repulsive is the word you meant to use?"

"Undeniably." She said dryly.

"You know I could have you dead for saying such a thing to me."

"And if you were going to, you would have done so by now," she added finally taking interest in the selections of tea. "I'm not scared of death, therefor, I'm not scared of you."

"There are worse things than death," I added, taking interest in her selection of teas. This entire setting was too much even for me. The herbs were disgusting, and my cup of blood was already going cold.

"The only thing that is worse than death is defying it," she said looking up at me.

"You mean becoming a vampire. Tell me, why does the daughter of Captain to our Wall Guard hate the monsters that she is protecting so much?" This was nice. Entertaining the novelty of pretending to care how a human mind functioned.

"Unlike some, I've come to terms with the monsters we live amongst and work for. What I can't justify is that we are trapped within these walls." I could relate to that. I hated when the walls first went up and my discovery of the world was left to bleed. I could leave at any time but found small pits of entertainment amongst this establishment until I grew too bored of it. Beyond the walls were the same. We were limited and I had already travelled all there was to see.

"We provide you safety from other Kingdoms that might not treat you so well. Humans wouldn't survive on their own for a week out there." There were rebel vampires who didn't belong to any one Kingdom. They would seek them out within days if they ventured on their own outside.

"And yet we're the ones guarding your walls and protecting *you*," she said sitting forward to lean over the table. I replicated her movement, so we were nose to nose.

"And it's our reputation that keeps majority of them away in the first place. Do you really think you'd be safe without the monsters that slept within the wall? No one would dare challenge us. And if they do, I can kill them singlehandedly. Not your party of humans who think so highly of themselves."

"That's rich coming from you," she seethed.

"Your majesty," one of the servants cleared his throat to

draw my attention. I snarled irritated that he had interrupted. This conversation was just becoming heated. Sasha reclined back into her chair. "They are ready."

Well, that put a smile on my face. "Well little mouse, show me what you can do. I've acquired five interior guards, all of which are vampire of course. They are average at best; I want to see how efficient my human bodyguard is."

"You want me to show you *how* I fight?" she asked almost insulted.

"Is five too much? I can make it less?" Humans were naturally weaker in every aspect opposed to a vampire. They had all the odds against them which is why I was so curious as to whether this little mouse had the right to speak so confidently. It didn't take long for her to take my bait and prepare to showcase why she was so bold. Servants pushed back the table and chairs so I could comfortably watch from a distance with my cup and pinkie poised.

I thought that the guards would take her less seriously, but it was the opposite. They seemed determined to kick her ass. They were told well in advance that none of them were to bite or kill her. If any of them stepped out of my instruction, I would kill all five. They were allowed to rough her up, sure why not.

"Sasha, Darling, if it gets all a little too much just wave your white flag, okay?" I antagonized. She ignored me as she collected the two swords from her back. She had other weapons that decorated her muscular frame. She swung them around having a feel for their weight and how they glided.

"Oh wait!" I said as they circled her and halted at my command. I held a gong and for theatrical suspense waited before I hit it. Couldn't miss an opportunity for flare. As soon as I hit it the vampires pounced. My heart would've beat frantically in anticipation if it hadn't stopped doing so long ago. I was exhilarated to see her fight.

She swung her sword at the first one, forcing them to step back. They didn't, instead, they glided their hands down the blade to grab it and fling it away. She let it go to avoid being pulled along with it. With unexpected speed, she jabbed her second sword into the woman's stomach and sliced it along. I laughed as the vampire's guts fell onto the floor. Her weapons were sharp and perfected to fight against vampires. A perfectly thinned silver blade, that if used correctly could easily kill our kind. The vampire shrieked and collected her guts from the floor.

Sasha skidded through the blood avoiding the advancing two that had already pounced towards her. *She was fast.* I furrowed my eyebrows. Too fast for a human to be able to match their pace and track their movement. Was she predicting their movement, is that how she was gliding through them so effortlessly?

The second vampire hammered down a sword over her; she protected herself with the might of one arm, her leather producing a small blade on the side of her extended arm. She was strong, too strong for a human to be able to match a vampire single handily. "Hmmm," I hummed to myself. Looks like my caged bird just became a lot more interesting.

With her other hand she sliced at its ankles in a swift movement, dropping it to the ground. She flicked its sword away and slit its throat open as it dropped to its knees. Blood splattered across her face. She flicked her piggy tail over her shoulders and there it was; what was once her brown eyes now entirely black, frenzied in a killing spree. *Now that I wasn't expecting.* For all that control and steely tongue of hers, it seemed that this little mouse was a killing machine and far from an ordinary human.

With rage and inhuman strength, she grabbed a dagger from her thigh and harpooned it towards one of the vampire's chest. It narrowly missed and pinned it to one of the nearby trees. *Very not human strength.* Had it been any closer to the heart she would've killed that vampire and I wasn't entirely certain she missed on purpose.

One of the vampires jumped on her back and held her in a choke hold, had it been under other circumstances they would've already bitten into her neck. But under my command the woman was not permitted to do so. The last standing man lurched towards her while she was pinned.

Sasha flicked the woman over her shoulder, crashing her on top of the man. She pulled a thin chain of silver out from her back sleeve and wrapped it around the woman's throat. She cleanly and precisely sliced it through the woman's neck beheading her.

The woman's head rolled onto the ground and her corpse slumped and began rotting. The other vampires paused momentarily. "You killed her!" The man behind her decaying body said. He flicked its dead weight off and charged Sasha. She wasn't coherent. She was on edge like an animal instinctually fighting to survive.

So technically she wasn't allowed to kill anyone, and it was an issue. But personally, I found it rather entertaining and liked the ending. Either way my little pet just caused me some serious issues. "Okay that's enough, Sasha Darling," I said clapping my hands together. I had seen enough. There was mystery behind the girl who wasn't entirely human. She held a lack of restraint like a wild dog. No wonder her father hadn't brought her to meet my brother sooner. I had never noticed her amongst the city before but how was such a creature living amongst us. My curiosity piqued, if not human, then what was she? I had never come across such an oddity.

She went to jump on the female vampire that was still attempting to collect her guts from the floor. With lightning speed, I grabbed Sasha by the throat and hung her in the air. She kicked and tried to thrash at me a few times, but my arm was extended far enough for her to do any real damage. She snarled at me, and I was immediately aroused. Watching the swirl of her darkness so evidently was like watching a painting develop. I knew she would be a masterpiece. Those blank black eyes that couldn't focus on anything at all was like gazing at the stars that held millions of possibilities of a world outside our own.

"Sasha," I growled huskily, entirely turned on by the situation. None of the other vampires stepped forward. She was my pet and no one was to interrupt how I treated my mouse. This was now a monster talking to a monster as I tried to call her back to her cage. "Unless you are trying to seduce me and want me buried inside of you, you need to control your shit." I clicked in front of her face. I didn't know if her eyes were following the movement because there were no pupils tracing my steps. But her thrashing slowly ceased. Just like a wild animal. I continued to click until I saw the brown come back to her eyes and her pupils returned. She took a gasp and I realized that she couldn't breathe while I held up her by the throat. I dropped her onto the ground and turned my back on her. She was no threat to me.

I turned to face the others who were pacing back and forth wanting to attack her again. When they walked in here they wanted to kick her ass. Perhaps her abnormality was general knowledge amongst the soldiers. There was communication between both human and vampire guards. Had they known who or what she was already? "This match is done," I said wiping away a smudge of blood that was on my suit. I had dressed up just for this occasion.

"But she killed one of our own!" One of them exclaimed. "There are rules against that!" I peered down on him. My presence alone cloaking and choking any further words he might say.

"*I* make the rules," I growled. "And no one is to touch what is *mine*. Understand?" I continued to look down on them so the distance grew wider between our superiority. No one was to defy me. "Clean this up," I hissed at the carcass that was melting and decomposing of rotten flesh.

"And where do you think you're going?" I demanded of Sasha as she packed up few of her things and went to leave the room.

"I have to go," she said hurriedly.

"But that's boring," I said stepping in front of her and blocking her path from the door.

"I showed you what you wanted to see," she seethed. Despite her steely demeanor her body reeked of fear. I took a step back baffled by the human emotion. Gross. So sensitive.

"But I have so many questions," I chimed trying to lighten the mood.

"I need to go," is all she said and she pushed past me.

"If you don't stay here under my protection, they will come after you for killing one of their own," I said behind her. She continued to walk away. I had no doubt she was already aware of that. Despite my warnings and threats they would come for her. A part of her probably hoped they did. With my entertainment gone for the day I decided for the first time ever to hit the library and records room to see what information I could muster on this far from human woman. The librarian had a near heart attack at me imposing on his sacred space. The fact that it was me of all people entering caused him concern. I had never stepped into this place. I wanted to see if I could find any records or description of this little mouse's past. Something was certainly amiss.

CHAPTER 3

HICKORY DICKORY HUNT

ESPITE THREATENING THE LIBRARIAN NUMEROUS times and flicking his ridiculous top hat off, he still couldn't find any further records on my little Sasha Pierce. The only significant thing on record was her father's hierarchy amongst the humans and guard over the wall. There was only mention of Sasha and her mother. There was a birth certificate, now twenty-eight and mention of her current respected ranking on the wall. That was it. The same for her mother. I wasn't at all surprised though, humans were rarely archived in our library. They didn't hold any great significance and didn't live very long, comparatively to our vampire lives. They died within what felt like a snap of the fingers. The only few humans that would receive more than dot points on their archives were the human rulers and cities that we overrun and overruled.

History was boring when you were a part of every

expedition. It was nothing more than a pastime and now we only had one another to overrule. I enjoyed those killings and blood sprees. Once we had fully dominated humans, I wasn't permitted to unleash my wrath like usual. My Father didn't condone my self-expression and glee in the arts of gory entertainment. Especially if it opposed his agenda. I was only allowed to kill on his command. Blah Blah Blah. I still did what I wanted but the nagging I received afterwards put me in a stupor. There had been times when he had tried to kill me. Not him personally but at his approval. They all failed.

Yet, my father always found a use for me. He would let me unleash on his enemies and then reel me back in as if taking a child away from its newfound toy. Oh, how I kicked and screamed. Meanwhile my brother was his scholar, his son with a keen eye who learnt all that he could from him like a sponge. Combined, the two were utterly boring. There were many times when my Father destroyed my new playthings. No matter who, what or project it was, he'd destroy it before I grew bored of it organically. He was always making a point that he was our overrule. So, unapologetically, that's why I killed him.

I slipped through one of the back gates that fenced the oversized grounds, closest to my private villa. The villas had originally been built for the royal family, now only housing my brother and me. There were another two smaller ones on the grounds that hadn't been entered for years. They were all positioned closely to the castle which was the symbol and core of my brother's ruling as King. I dipped into the castle from time to time when I was truly bored hoping to disturb the politicians and scholars that followed my brother everywhere.

The guards on watch acknowledged me as I walked past but said nothing as I stalked across the green grounds. Everything here was lavish and well maintained. Thinking back on the old days was forcing me in dire desperation to get out of this pen once again. If it hadn't been for the mention of a possible upcoming war, I would've left sooner. But if the fun was to be at my very own home than that's where I would be.

It was six months ago that my brother announced the inclination that our neighboring kingdom that was ruled by King Oppollo might attempt to break down our walls. I danced in glee at the prospect. It was true that we had a formidable line of resources and best of all had a glorious number of humans to feed on. Admittedly I didn't help that cause with my lack of control, but my brother made sure to compensate their families if I went a little extreme and accidently killed the livestock. We were to live harmoniously with them. Drink their blood and repay them with their houses and jobs and blah blah blah. I didn't care for the system, but my brother did.

I prayed that Oppollo tried to break down our walls and steal from us. Finally, some bloodshed that I wouldn't be reprimanded for. Since then my brother had been playing the boring means of political games and tact. I personally just wanted to burn their entire Kingdom to the ground. I'd attempted to leave twice now, but my brother had Galador trailing me like I was a virgin girl out on the city for the first night, to make sure I didn't do anything stupid. So, I waited, as patiently as I ever had in my life, waiting for the signal to burn them to the ground.

I was absolutely humming now to have found Sasha who would be my new toy until the war began. It should tick over some time until I found my fun elsewhere again. I circled the fencing and outskirts of the castle and began my hunt. I inhaled, heightening my senses to focus on that one coppery yet floral scent. Feminine mixed with a steely masculinity.

I sifted through the many scents that passed through the

entrance of the castle that day. The surrounding flowers tried to intercept my sense of keen smell. The artificial day began to dim turning into night. I looked forward to a hunt that would be overshadowed by moonlight. Bingo. I found her scent and charmed a wicked smile. And so, the hunt would begin.

I would find my little mouse wherever she scurried away to hide. I wanted answers as to why she could match the speed and strength of a vampire and her eyes dilated into blackness. The thought of it aroused me once again. My cock throbbed uncomfortably in my pants at the thought. I'd had vampire lovers who had lost control, usually youngsters, but it was nothing more than a tantrum or fight and flight response. But her movement was controlled, greedy, and deadly. She was a human weapon. That excited me and I wanted to know why she was so different. I was certain it was why I was attracted to her unusual blend of metallic and floral scent that I'd never smelt before. I wanted to dig my fangs as deep as my cock inside of her.

I darted through the clean streets within the city of Grand Klaus. A rather outdated name in my opinion but my brother denied my idea of titling the city after myself. As I followed the scent it took me further into the human compounds and apartments. The vampires and humans often stuck to their own species only overlapping for the night scene and parties for the humans who felt daring. The architect of the designated areas was vastly different. While the humans enjoyed their flowers and modern white walls with bright lights, the vampires had bricked buildings and gothic theme. Majority of the vampires within this city were younger, less than a few hundred years old. I remembered going through that gothic, eerie stage as well. I tsked at myself for the audacious and flamboyant attire I would wear. Though I looked dashing no matter what I wore.

Those who were older had a sense of finery and nobility to them. They could afford to live closer to the castle with more perks. A lot of those residents had been fighters from the last war who followed my Father to overthrow this region's human leaders and outside vampires that tried to overthrow our victory. It was an easy way to keep a closer eye on them. If anyone was daring enough to have alternative ambitions or want to overthrow my brother, then I was permitted to discard of them in whatever way I felt necessary. I was the reaper after all. It had acquired me some entertainment these last few months as I stalked them separately. There was speculation that someone from the inside of the walls was feeding information to Oppollo. I relished in the fun as these old warriors were looking over their shoulder as they went about their daily business. It was amazing to watch what paranoia could do to an immortal when their mortality was being questioned.

The streets reeked of all kinds of humans. Like a herd of cattle that had been unchecked for a while living in their own passive lives. Despite the unattractive scenery route, I was exhilarated to stalk Sasha. I anticipated to see her again even though it had only been a few hours since I had seen her last.

I stalked through the outer edges of one region which was sketchier than most. Less humans housed in the buildings as they had vacated for the more modern style towards the inner city. The apartment building was three stories high and was a mixture of the old gothic brick layered style with a modern twist. There was a small swimming pool on the top floor with glass roofing that I could barely see through. The pool had gone green and the windows looked as if they hadn't been cleaned for decades.

I took another whiff. Sasha was definitely inside. I ascended the building next to me so I could sit across from her apartment building and simply watch. When I settled myself into position, I realized I was perched beside a golden cross. Dear God. I looked around the grounds that I sat on and the sign below me that read 'church' with a quote from the bible on the dusty board.

I laughed, I forgot they had these funny things and still prayed. "Remember back in the day when they thought your name and buildings kept us away?" I said shaking my finger into the sky. I personally wasn't a believer but hey stranger things have happened and if there was a God, he was a merciless bastard to let us monsters roam his human's world.

Every priest within the city of Grand Klaus was a vampire. A safety measure by my brother to ensure no rebellion of sorts occurred by using God's name or instruction in vein. "Well fuck me, I do listen," I said baffled that even I knew that. "I've been in this city for too long."

I crouched, still as a gargoyle beside the cross. My suit jacket flapped in the wind ever so slightly from time to time. I could sense her walking around in her apartment. I could only sense another two residents within the building. Much to my luck, she entered the unused pool room and began to train where I could so clearly see her. Strike one, strike two on the dummy with stealth.

I watched her, transfixed as she trained for two hours and then sat down cross legged and sweaty to sharpen her blades. Nightfall was upon us and there was a slight temperature change. I knew that by the few humans who walked past with jackets on. Despite the darkness I could still see her clearly. I enjoyed watching her every movement and predatory state that seemed constantly on edge.

I caught a whiff of something wicked coming this way. Vampires jumped from building to building to close in on her apartment complex. I sighed disheartened by how predictable they were. *'Let's grab our pitchforks and kill the human that killed one of our own, blah blah blah.'*

I stood up, anticipating their arrival. Eight of them. All for one puny human. How shameful. Like a bunch of thugs ganging up on somebody for something trivial. Well, at least this would cause some entertainment for the night. I took two steps back to give me a little running distance. I lurched forward and fell onto her apartment rooftop silently so I could counter the oncoming vampires. As I stood another vampire couldn't change his course after jumping from the previous building. I caught him by the throat before his feet even touched the tiles. I ripped out his jugular with disdain. There was a gurgling noise before I dropped his filthy and gasping remains on the floor. I dusted off my jacket feeling filthy after the contact.

The fellow seven vampires skidded to a silent halt on the rooftop. They all immediately recognized who I was and shit themselves.

"I specifically recall stating that the human was mine," I said flicking away black blood that had begun to run down my hand. The vampire held his throat, uncomfortable by the open wound. He didn't need to breath, but it would take some time to heal.

"Your Majesty," one of the young girls with black short hair dropped to her knee.

"None of that," I said. I sensed Sasha directly beneath me. There was a thick amount of grime on the glass roofing that we stood on. It might've been difficult to see clearly but she knew that we were there. She probably anticipated a barrage of vampires like this to come after her.

"I could kill you all in seconds but then there would be no fun in that," I chimed. Fear scattered their faces and one had the audacity to try and run.

With speed that outmatched his, I countered him before he jumped off the roof. I punctured through his spine and ripped his heart from behind. Immediately his body began to decay. I looked at his rotten heart with disgust. So gross yet delightfully beautiful. Transfixed as always, I tried to focus on my objective.

"Right, sorry, I forgot you were here," I said with a smile and turned around to the others. "Here, a souvenir," I said throwing the heart over to one of his companions. They caught it unknowing of what to do with it. "Let's play a little game and you all really have *no* choice but to stay. Like this guy," I pointed to the decaying gross carcass as I kicked it over the edge of the building and watched it splat on the ground. I giggled to myself. "Don't be this guy."

"A… A game?" The woman with short black hair stumbled. Finally, one that had the courage to at least speak. I offered her a reassuring crazed smile.

"Yes, a game. It's rather simple. No one is allowed to leave this rooftop building. You will fight one another until only one remains. That vampire will be rewarded by me personally."

I felt Sasha slowly prowl underneath. She was anticipating the attack that would never come. Not tonight anyways. I was right to believe that fun would follow her. I didn't recognize any of these brats. None of them worked within the castle which meant someone inside had orchestrated this little band and objective. And someone besides my brother giving out orders would not do.

"You want us to kill each other?" One of the taller men said. His fangs indicated he was no more than fifty years old. They were babies. My, how messy this fighting would be. Unskilled and desperate. My favorite.

"Yes, well it's rather simple if even the brawn of the

group understood. So, without further ado…" I flashed through them with lightning speed and rested against the chimney so I could comfortably lean and cross my legs. "On the count of three, begin." I offered an enthusiastic smile. They looked at one another, uncertain. Their independent nature would kick in. Fight or flight. My favorite. "Three, two, one, go!" I said fast.

Without hesitation all of them dove into the center. At the click of my fingers they fought one another. There was no choice and no place for them to run. I could torture and kill them all myself in seconds if I wanted to. This was their only chance of survival and that's why they fought. Such weak little monsters.

Blood splattered this way and that for minutes until the job was done. I was impressed by some of the maneuvers. Others were clumsy mistakes that cost them their lives. Six carcasses rotted on the rooftop, the wind picking up the stench and throwing it towards the city. The victor was the woman with black short hair. I clapped in theatrical approval. Not bad for a youngster.

"Now, who sent you?" I asked, no longer leaning against the chimney. She looked down at her previous comrades before that selfish glaze washed over her face. She didn't care about the loss. We were accustomed to faking human presence and emotion.

"Only Petar received the location. We were told by him that we'd get a chance to work within the castle walls," she admitted. She wasn't lying. I had a keen sense for when I was being lied to.

"Who is Petar?" I asked. She pointed to the closest carcass near me. *Ah, the tall brawny one.* "I probably should've asked that question as a group first." I took mental note of the mistake. I looked down into the pool area. It would've been so much more convenient if Sasha were in there bathing. Instead of a green pool I envisioned a hot tub. At least we could've watched this grand spree of murder happen together. "Well, girl, or whatever your name is, your reward is that you can now break in through this window," I pointed to the glass window that I was standing on. Precisely the spot that I sensed Sasha standing beneath. "And have at it with the human. That way you will still get the reward, right?"

Her eyebrows furrowed. "But you said she was yours?" She said confused.

"Well yes, and she is. But it'll be fun for me to watch. So, don't do it yet. Wait until I'm standing back over there," I pointed to the cross that I had perched next to above the church previously. "And when I give you the thumbs up you can jump in, so I can watch." I gave her a smile and without further conversation leapt over the distance. I wanted to see this play out from the side. I lightly touched down in my previous spot and waited with glee. I took a step to the left and then a step to the right, trying to achieve the best angle where I could see all the fighting.

I angled my fingers to create a frame and drifted it back and forth. *Yes, I think this spot is best.* Smash. Before I could even give the vampire thumbs up to jump in, Sasha broke through the glass from the pool room and ended her within seconds. I dropped my finger frame utterly guttered. There wasn't even a real fight.

She looked at the massacre of decaying bodies on the roof and then looked in my direction—directly at me. Caught in the act I simply waved with a heartfelt warm smile. She pulled out a gun and shot an arrow towards me. I grabbed it before it hit its target, my heart. I began to laugh, cackling in delight. Oh, my she was a fiery one.

I wavered the arrow in her direction. "Alright, Sasha Darling, I'll see you tomorrow then!" And as giddy as a teenage boy I jumped off the roof and onto the next, skipping my way back home. I doubted that anyone else would attack her tonight. Her apartment building would now reek of me and eight dead vampires. A message that no one was to attempt to touch what I had already declared as mine.

As I sped on the rooftops and back home, I looked down at the arrow that was meant for my heart. I charmed a wicked smile. *I think she likes me.*

CHAPTER 4

KYRAN HAS HIMSELF A PET

"How is it that I've been gone for only four days and yet," my brother said as way of entering the room and flicking my inclined feet off the edge of the armchair in our reading room. "You cause so much mayhem. Look at this room, show some restraint."

"Come now, Amell, don't be such a sourpuss," I said dropping the girl's bloody wrist from my face. I was sprawled out in our reading room. It was decorated with wooden and polished furniture and a black marble fireplace. It was where Amell often read books and I would from time to time pester him.

This time, instead of walking into his peaceful and boring space, he was greeted by three women and two men near unconscious from blood loss and well, perhaps I was a bit messy. Fresh blood stained the furniture and seeped through the lush white carpet. In my defense, the fire still crackled untouched and that was the only descent feature in this room. I was doing him a favor. "Take a seat, I've missed you."

He shook his head, as he always did with a disapproving glare. We shared similar features but he looked a few years older. He was however slightly less attractive, shorter, less muscular, boring, and lacked charm.

He stepped over the two unconscious naked men shaking his head and grumbling under his breath. Instead of taking a seat in his usual corner piece, he opted to lean against the fireplace. Besides beheading, taking our heart out, and stabbing us with silver; fire was one natural element that could kill us. And yet as the devils we were, we liked to watch it, bewildered by the very thing that could end us finally.

"It seems like you've been busy in the short time that I've been gone," he said in his smooth, velvety voice. Even his manner of clothing was different to mine. I preferred to be somewhat fashionable—he enjoyed dressing like a boring middle-aged man only now figuring out that he could have more than one color in his wardrobe. I wondered how much of that was Galador's fault considering I was near certain he had been dressing him for as long as I could remember.

"I wouldn't call myself busy, rather the opposite. I've been rather bored," I said honestly pushing away the woman who was still trying to cling to me for more. Humans were so weak in their resolve. As soon as they get a little bite, boom they're jacked up on endorphins and want more until they are bled dry. Of course, I could control that if I wanted. You could make the experience as sensational or as traumatizing for them. "Get off me," I said pushing her to the side. She flopped to the ground giddy. She began to lick at her own wound. I scrunched my face up. "Filthy little wench," I rasped.

Amell just watched me, as he always did with those

calculating blue eyes. He never looked at me predatory like. After I killed our father, the realization that I was considerably stronger overshadowed how people acted around me. In a sick and twisted way his murder answered their silent questions. Amell was built for paperwork and I was best for killing. He wouldn't dare raise a hand or argue against me, he was too calculating for that. I wished he would though, which was why I tormented him so much. I wanted to see how my big brother would play with me.

"I've been advised that you've taken interest in one of the human wall watchers," he began. He continued to stare at me. I was certain that my brother would be the champion of staring competitions. "And that you allowed her to kill one of our own in these very walls and you killed another eight who pursued her afterwards?"

One of the men on the floor moaned. Amell's eyes diverted to him in disgust for disrupting him. I let out a sigh. *Someone was in a poopy mood.* I clicked at the servant who silently stood against the wall. He creeped from the shadows and began tumbling the humans out. Within seconds they were gone. The door clicked behind him leaving my wishy-washy boring brother and me alone. *Well thank God I had my dinner before this little meltdown.*

"Galador is such a snitch." I grabbed a silk napkin and wiped the few droplets of blood that was around my mouth. "I didn't kill any vampires. Wait no, that's a lie. I only killed one. And that was after I told them not to pursue Sasha. And then six of them killed each other. And then Sasha killed the last one. In all fairness its rather shameful that a tiny human can kill so many. They were meant for the grave if a little human can-"

"Kyran! I am trying to create order here!" He said cutting me off. I charmed a smile. Maybe this would turn into something of a fight.

"Order has always been your monopoly brother. Not mine."

He tsked me and began to pace making me near nauseous on a full belly. "You know that there is a world beyond these walls that could destroy the very future we are trying to create for ourselves," he began with his usual speech.

"It's so boring, Brother. Instead of hiding ourselves amongst the few kingdoms surrounding us, we should be ransacking them and taking the entirety of this world. I don't understand what's so hard to comprehend about that." We had for the longest of times acknowledged that there was a world beyond the one that we lived in. There was a parallel world of different origin, where humans lived alone without our kind. This place of our existence was not our final destination, we just had to figure out how to enter the new world. Until then, we were stuck in our own dome like existence and small terrain that had us fighting over land and resources.

That was the focus of my father and brother's time, to tactfully migrate into the new world 'safely.' Not mine, I found the whole process rather boring and would rather bust through and announce myself as their new Fairy Godfather.

"You know it's not that easy!" Amell growled frustrated. It was the embarrassment of his team to have not yet figured out how to escape into this otherworld. Sure, we had to go where the humans and livestock were. But everything had to be done 'safely.' What if we couldn't survive there? What if it was so vastly different? What if we would combust upon walking through the magical gates? Blah Blah. Whine. They were no closer to finding where the entrance was let alone the precautionary of such a mission.

We were so limited in our thinking and ability to get there. It was such a fantasy if it were even real. The story of this world had begun and was passed down from the humans claiming that they had been abducted and brought to this place. That was going back to before a time any of us could remember. Few humans had slipped in throughout the years wearing strange clothes and with no understanding of our world or how they came to be. They thought themselves dead and in Hell. Who knew, maybe this was their Hell. So, it made me beg the question why we weren't overthrowing and taking the major throne? I had no care to be a king of such a place but I did want to fight and kill to get there. We either conquered here or skipped into a new world with a bigger challenge and more livestock to shed through.

"I'm just saying there is no guarantee you or I will live for that long, Brother, so we might as well enjoy the time that we have," I said. We very rarely spoke between ourselves of the new world. We viewed it differently. To believe in something that we had never seen. He took a seat across from me and crossed his legs in contemplation. My brother cared too much about the meaning of our existence. We were monsters. That was it. Nothing more. Top of the food chain. We didn't need to think any further in the matter and how we came about.

He grunted to change the subject. "This new fascination of yours, the wall watcher–"

"Sasha," I interrupted to correct him. I had recently upgraded her from toy to thing with a name. He watched me cautiously for a moment longer. He was probably surprised that I remembered the title of another living creature for once. I didn't much care for remembering people's names because usually they were boring.

"Is it Sasha Pierce?" He asked very calculated.

"Why, yes Big Brother, that's my little mouse. Do you know her?" I asked for the first time, very interested in what my brother had to say during this conversation.

"I've worked with her father closely a few times. I keep reports on them, specifically the daughter after the incident with his wife," he said ominously. It was an oppressive side to my brother. He really nailed the solitary lone soldier act. He pointed at me when I didn't change my expecting expression for him to continue with the story. "Of which I already told you the details twenty years ago. But of course, you weren't listening. This is why I stopped conversing with you on such matters!"

"Well yes, I'm sure you said it in an uninteresting way, but now I'm interested." I prompted him to continue.

"The girl is strange," he said in a different thought.

"Yes, I'm aware." And yet that oddity had my cock throbbing at the thought. The vision of her steely like gaze had me stroking my bottom lip. I thought about the way she shot that arrow at me, ahh. I dropped to my knees and held my brother's hands. I looked up at him adoringly for the answers that I wanted. "Tell me more."

He shook his head unamused by my theatrics. He threw off my hand and looked away, disgusted. "Her mother was a scientist. Her result was experimenting on Sasha and other children who watch the wall in Sashsa's team. She had an ideal to mix vampire with human. Not like we would turn a human. She wanted to craft humans who could match the speed and stamina of vampires. She had an ideal to take back humanity with these—Hunters.

When Sasha's father discovered the live experiments, he reported it to me immediately. When we were to catch her, she had disappeared. No one knows where she went to this day. We considered killing the children but with madness came results. The children were different, stronger, and faster. So now they work at the wall under our rule and thumb. We watch them closely to make sure that there is no uprising of her mother's ideals. Our own have been studying them ever since."

I hummed over that. How fascinating. So little Sasha was her mother's personal Guinea pig. How illusive. And I would say that little Sasha darling was far more than a teeny tiny bit stronger and faster. She could match the speed of vampires rather exceptionally. "Is that where the scar came from?" I asked envisioning the jagged scar that ran down her neck.

"I don't know about any scar," he added. "It's been a while since I've seen her father. I might call upon him in the next few days for a report on any changes. Strange that she would come here herself. She's never been in the castle to address me personally before."

"Well you talk to dear old daddy while I try to fuck his daughter," I said patting his hand and standing up to leave. That's all I needed to know; the angle of the chat was starting to turn into a serious notion. My brother always got a glaze about him when he was being serious.

"Don't you want to know how my visit with Calabar went?" he asked as I went to leave. Calabar was a broody vampire and boring. He wasn't a King but was a leader to a large group of rogues and bandits outside the wall. My brother wanted to make sure that if necessary, he had reinforcements if Oppollo would try to overthrow him in the next few months. So much sitting around and waiting because of he said, she saids.

"Unless we are going to war with someone tomorrow, I don't care," I said honestly and made way for the door. Until then, I still had an unquenchable thirst that not even draining five humans could nullify. The predatory side of me wanted to yet again go on a hunt. And with night upon me once again, I couldn't think of anything better than to take my new pet out for a stroll.

CHAPTER
5

INTO THE WILD THEY STROLL

I HAD ONCE READ OF a romantic notion that a boy threw
pebbles at a girl's window to endearingly grab her
attention during the night. She was inundated with surprise
and then glee that he had thought of her and come to see
her unannounced. I could woo Sasha with such a human
notion. I stood outside her window with pebble in hand.
"Now if I just gently throw this." I flicked it with as little
force as I could. The small rock chipped through and
smashed the window into obliteration with consequential
force. A booby trap was triggered, and arrows shot out of
the wall from eleven different directions.

I skidded left and right dodging them in the fun of the
game. Well hot damn, was this woman overly cautious when
it came to security. After avoiding the barrage of arrows that
were meant to murder me, I looked up and met her stealthy
brown eyes through the broken window. She held a gun

poised in my direction, unimpressed. She could fire as many of those arrows as she wanted, and it wouldn't do a damn thing. Maybe amateur vampires but not me.

"What do you want Kyran?" She asked irritated and put the gun down.

"I was just passing through the neighborhood randomly," I said circling my finger and admiring my surroundings. "And thought perhaps you'd like to take a walk outside the walls with the most handsome vampire you've ever laid eyes on?" I was certain she couldn't resist. I knew that she wanted nothing more than to see outside and past the walls. She wouldn't have asked for an audience and permission otherwise. I was curious as to whether her pride would hold her back from taking hold of my generous opportunity.

She was wearing a short sleeve shirt and black underwear. No lace. Entirely boring but the cream of her legs made me consider another proposition. *Why go outside the walls when we could stay in. And when I say in, I mean inside of her.* She huffed in disapproval as if having read my mind. Her hair wasn't in its usual poised pinned back ponytail. It was messy like a wild animal. An untamed mane that was entirely appropriate for this beast of a woman. "Or perhaps I could come join you in that cold apartment beside that cold beating heart of yours? Maybe I could warm you up from the inside?"

"Is this anything but a game to you?" She asked, pissed off now. How I loved to see that glow of hatred simmer on her face. Because hatred was the definition of passion. Both were wild and irrational. I knew it would be only a matter of time until I could convert that dire need to kill me to transfix into the desire to fuck me. I'd never had to wait this long before, it was all rather exhilarating.

"Everything is but a game, Darling. Play with me?" I purred, reaching out my hand to her in dramatic flare and welcoming gesture. "Or I will take what I desire forcefully." My charming threat didn't force her to deter that steely gaze.

"I could kill you; you know? Actually end your existence," she said with absolute certainty. I scoffed and laughed looking around to see if anyone else was here to listen to the hilarious joke she had made. Of course, no one else was around. Just us. No, I doubted little Sasha had many friends in her neighborhood with an attitude like that. Nobody even stirred at the commotion from the mass shooting of arrows that had come my way. When I honed in on my hearing, I noted Sasha Darling still only had two fellow humans' hearts beating. My, those must have been daring tenants.

"Didn't you want to go beyond the walls? I thought I would permit your little request without the rest of your little classmates to tag along. Come and play with teacher for a little bit," I said with a creepy suggestive smile. No matter what I said or insisted on her, this woman didn't shudder in fear or budge in submission. If anything, her venomous tongue that I permitted to speak, rapidly spat back. "I won't leave here."

"I will howl all night if I have to," I added in splendid humor. I was not one to lose games. Ever.

She seethed under her breath and receded back into the shadows of her home. Minutes later she came out the front door with her long golden hair tied up. *Always the military enforcer.* She wore black leather pants with a few weapons strapped to her thighs including the usual two swords strapped to her back.

"Oh, you won't need those Darling, I'll protect you of course," I said to antagonize her. I knew full well that Sasha

Pierce could look after herself. Well, she would die trying to do so.

"I was considering sharpening them on your tongue," she replied. I howled out a laugh at her deadpan humor. When, oh when would I have this woman smile and laugh at me? Did she cackle as wickedly as I imagined her to? Could she moan as softly as I desired her to? My cock twitched at the thought. I was entirely transfixed by this little mouse. The entirety of my attention was fixated on her. Her scent swallowed me whole and I lavished in the smell with desire. I clenched my hands into fists acquiring restraint from reaching out to grab her. Control was not my strongest playing card and yet I wanted to toy with this new pet for as long as I could. Sooner or later I would likely accidently break it like all the others. So, for now I would enjoy the play.

"Why are you doing this?" She asked. "You know we aren't allowed to leave without permission." I strolled at a tremendously slow and human pace to keep up with hers. I wondered if she was purposefully walking at such a slow pace in hopes that I would become fed up and leave her before we even made it to the wall. She was so cunning in many ways.

"Is that the generosity you should be showing towards the very man that is giving you exactly what you want? I believe a thank you is in order."

"I don't see you as a man," she corrected. I chuckled.

"You will when I'm ten inches deep inside of you." I could hear the change in her heartbeat, until that steely control of hers held the reins once again. When she spoke, neither her tone nor body gave away any such inclination. If it weren't for the added benefits of being a vampire with sensitive hearing, I wouldn't have been any wiser to how she reacted at the mention of my ten-inch cock. Oh, how my tightly controlled little human didn't like to give anything away.

"I would never let you fucking come ten miles near me," she said. I chuckled at that. Listening to my little Sasha say filthy words was nothing short of a tease.

"You're only human my Dear; Curiosity is what both makes and destroys your kind. You'll want a taste and when you do, there will be no going back." I purred adamantly looking down on her from the corner of my eye. She would come to the dark side. Someone who already had a monstrous nature within them was a ticking time bomb in this world. Power always thirsted for power. "It's inevitable."

"Do you know what the downfall of your kind is?" She asked rhetorically.

"Our good looks and charm that can't be overlooked?" I replied earnestly.

"Your arrogance of superiority will be your downfall. It'll kill you all," she said deadpan. I hummed at that as if contemplating. *Wow, she was intense. I wondered if she knew what the term 'flirting' meant.*

"My Darling, it was humans who had crumbled because of their own oversite and short measures. Don't ever forget that you're guarding *our* walls and are *our* livestock. You were arrogant to believe that you could ever fight back–even with your technology." *I hope this conversation ends.*

"Or maybe you're nothing but an experiment built from humans in the other world which is why we've been cornered off into this plane. Maybe you're all being controlled without even realizing it," she responded as we neared the wall. I side eyed her again. *Well this seducing thing went very philosophical quick.* Most knew about the parallel world we lived in, but this was the only existence many of us knew. Did their world know about vampire's existence? Were they as technologically advanced as us? My brain fried and I scoffed at her. How dare she make me think this far ahead. I had no foresight, nor did I care until it was something I could strangle in front of me. She was an idealist just like Amell. *Why was I so cursed?*

"I don't care for 'how we came to be' conversations Sasha. They're rather boring."

"It's because you're so short-sighted," she seethed. I looked at her and noticed that her gaze was on the wall. No, beyond the wall picturing something that she so direly wanted. I looked at it and raised my eyebrows in dramatic consideration. Two soldiers stood on their post on alert by our approach to the side gate.

"No Darling, it's simply because I focus on the now. I don't age a bit. I'll move with the times inevitably. You won't, which is why you want so many answers in your short and tiny life to validate self-purpose. You humans are all the same." *How her young ideals disappointed me. Perhaps she was like the rest after all.* I walked towards the two humans who were smaller than me in size. They looked at Sasha and then me in confusion. I thought that we made a dashing couple.

"So… so… sorry Sir," the first male stumbled. "You can't go through the–"

"You know who I am, don't you," I said towering over him. He fumbled for words. The second, less spineless human spoke.

"You don't have clearance. Sasha–" he said looking around me to speak with her. I grabbed him by the throat and dangled him in the air. The other one unsheathed his weapons, timid and unknowing what to do. Sasha unsheathed her own swords behind me.

"Drop him, Kyran!" She said in a cold tone. Well at least she did see me for what I truly was. A threat.

"You're speaking with me, not her," I said to the man who tried to pry his own fingers from my steely grip. So weak. So feeble and pathetic. "Your friends need to learn some manners, my little mouse," I said over my shoulder to Sasha. Oh, how I wanted to break this man's neck. I crushed my pointed nails into his throat to watch the small streams of blood trickle down my fingers. How I missed the lavish sight of someone grasping with the idea that I might be their death. That dimming gleam of panic that their life might end but the uncertainty of what was to come in the afterlife. "Will it hurt, that's what you're wondering isn't it?" I cooed to the man. His eyes widened as he began to turn pale in the face. He continued to scratch at my hands desperately.

Oh, how these human guards thought they were so strong. Sasha ran at me from behind. There was a trickle of both excitement and betrayal all at once. I twisted and moved out of her way. Those vampires she took out might have been an equal match for her but I would never be such a thing. I drifted like smoke before her eyes and dropped the man behind her. Decidedly I kept him alive. The gates required two people to open them. He was useless to me dead. Either that or I broke through the gates, which I didn't mind. But I didn't want to listen to Galador pester at me and ruin my mood after my hot date.

I stood with my hands behind my back as if I had done nothing wrong. The man gasped beside me. I kicked him slightly which propelled him across the ground and into the gate. "Well, open the gate," ah, and then suddenly I realized why this had all gone wrong. I had to impress the lady after all. "Please." I added.

His spineless colleague helped him up. Sasha stepped in front of them with swords raised. I could never read her expression. I imagined it went along the lines of '*I never realized how big and strong he was.*' "Calm down little mouse," I said gesturing for her to lower the swords. "You're being slightly dramatic now." Her eyes narrowed on me. The two men scurried to open the gates. Well at least they followed instruction.

"Now as we were, our date," I gestured for her to step aside. "Now boys, I know that these little hidey holes can be opened like tiny little windows." I pointed to the dome panels. "I want one to be opened every night right above here," I said pointing to the dome that kept out the sun. "But it's to be kept as our little secret, okay?" I smiled and walked past them. I greeted Sasha with a wider smile as they rolled open the gates.

Lastly, I approached the scaredy cat of the two men who dared to say no to me. "If you tell anyone about this, I will not only kill you but the entirety of your family. I will also kill your bird. If you don't have a pet bird, I will gift you a pet bird and I will kill it. Wonderful chat," I said tapping him on the shoulder as he bleached white. I didn't look back at the other man as his filthy blood ensnared my nose. I wiped my bloody hands on his friend's metal clothing. My nails scratched along his armor and engrained marks as I wiped the blood clear.

"Come now Darling," I said posing as a gentleman. I walked past her, adjusting my unscathed leather jacket. Surely but steadily she followed me through the gates afterwards, sheathing her blades again.

"I'll explain later," she said to our onlookers. Ah, here goes the humans needing insight again. And there was nothing past the truth of what this was. A simple stroll outside the walls amongst soon to be lovers.

The outside was seemingly refreshing. Not that my body

felt such things as temperature change or breeze but the hairs on Sasha's arms rose which indicated it was colder beyond the walls. Her breathe expelled white mist as she wrapped her arms around herself. I looked at my jacket and then back at her. Perhaps I should make such a grand gesture.

"Don't even think about offering me your jacket," she said looking out and beyond. I chuckled as I followed her gaze. She would rather freeze to death than smell like me. How poetic. Her eyes thrilled with amazement. A long windy dirt path was before us. Our kingdom was amongst mountains, a difficult place to reach and with narrow entry points. If anyone decided to attack us, they would be at a disadvantage.

The trees rustled in the cold night and the half-moon shone down on us in blessing. It didn't look that different from the manufactured one inside the wall. Neither were seemingly spectacular. But I took another look in case I was missing something; because everything the little mouse looked at was in idle wonder.

"Have you never been outside the wall?" I asked as I kept my pace with hers. It wasn't as slow as it had been inside. Now she was taking long steps. She would kneel down to study certain plants in wonder. She'd rub them and sniff them. Rip some out by their roots and place them in her pocket. I watched her trivially. How could one person find so much excitement in a plant that was half dormant from the cold?

"Only once with my Father," she said ripping another plant out of the ground. Had others been around I may have had to kill them for mocking her odd behavior. But to me, it was interesting to watch. I couldn't predict her next move or what she was thinking. A novelty amongst not only my race but humans as well.

"Where is your Father?" I asked. I was still expecting a strongly worded letter from the man who should be concerned that I've taken interest in his daughter. Unless he was as loyal to my brother's throne as most of the boring humans.

"He's around," she said. "We're just waiting for you to permit us all to leave the walls instead of just favoring me." She didn't even look at me as she began scouting another noise. Evidently, she was a natural hunter even outside the walls. She leaned her head closer to the ground to listen. I think. I couldn't understand why she was doing that odd movement. The large scar down her neck bulged and shone under the moonlight as she continued to tilt her head. Oh, how I wondered about that scar and its origin. Its jagged edges made her all so much more beautiful. Brutal and savage just like my darling here.

I could hear the very rodent she was tracking, scampering about for food. "Dear God, Sasha Darling, please don't try and touch that filthy thing," I said. She immediately shushed me.

After twenty minutes of trying to track it she looked at me with a hmph. "Help me catch it," she said.

"Ew, no," I raised my hand to her. "I'm not touching that filthy beast."

"Stop being a wimp and just do it," she said clearly frustrated by her own futile efforts. *Diabolical.* How could she sincerely ask *me* to help her catch a rodent? But then another passing thought crossed my mind. *As a woman, she's asking me as the burly man to help her and hunt for her.* Ah, yes. I see, well played Sasha, giving me the thumbs up to our childish flirting games. Within a flash of a second, I darted past her and found the filthy furry creature. I darted back with her prize ready to receive my reward.

"Here, my Lady," I said offering her the filthy rodent by the tail. It was oversized and slightly mutated from God knows what and smelling of some sort of nature abiding disease.

"You killed it!" She said starring at the dead rodent that swayed back and forth from the wind. I dropped it onto the ground in front of her feeling more like a house cat than a rewarded male.

"How dare you? How do you know it didn't kill itself?" I asked looking down on her as she crouched over the infested creature. She huffed but collected the dead rodent anyway. I grimaced as she touched it.

"Give me your jacket," she insisted. I raised my hand immediately.

"You are not using my jacket to hold a dead rodent in it!" *Had she no shame!*

"You don't even get cold. Now give it to me." After hesitation she added. "Please." I stared at her unblinking. The only time I was to receive manners from this diabolical woman was when she wanted to use my jacket as a blanket for a dead rodent. But I was a strong man. A powerful vampire. Such matters didn't affect me. I took off my jacket and offered it to her as the gift it was. I grimaced and looked away as she collected the rodent in it and tucked it under her arm. She looked up at the sky and began to walk towards the wall.

"We should go. Sunrise will be soon," she said. I was already aware that sunrise was soon and was willing to let this go on for a few minutes more. Never did I think that she would take my safety into consideration.

"Surely you're not taking that disgusting thing back in the walls?" I asked as she carried my scrunched jacket under her arm. Her own pocket was stuffed with random assortments of plants. *What in God's name was she going to do with all these things?*

She ignored me and continued walking towards the gates, those lovely hips swaying like no one's business. I had found myself the most unpredictable specimen yet.

"Lucky me," I grumbled under my breath and surprisingly she did look over her shoulder, if only to make sure that I was following her.

CHAPTER
6

DOWN THE RODENT HOLE WE GO

DAY AND NIGHT STROLLS WITH my Darling Sasha slid through the pinprick of time. I orchestrated the same cycle every day. She didn't think highly of my romantic notion. She became begrudging as I announced my presence on her doorstep every night. Despite her seething words she escorted me each time. We slipped through the open panel to escape the boundaries of the wall. No guard on duty dared to interfere as they turned a blind eye. We would idly chat but only when she chose to respond. She continued to collect odd bits and pieces without explanation as to why.

The following day, I would orchestrate the exact same loop. I was so transfixed that I couldn't even sleep during the day. I fed on and fucked others during the day, hoping that it would ease the tension that was straining my body. Instead of bringing her into the castle to toy with every day I allowed her a small dose of freedom. I watched her from afar as she went about her daily duties at the wall. My cock was rock hard as I watched her boss the others about.

It tempered me the way that some of our castle guards had looked at her. I was jealous at the thought of any other male grabbing her attention. I didn't want to go on a killing spree accidently in my brother's workplace after all. It was Galador who suggested that I keep her at the wall and watch her from afar during the day. Those weren't his specific words but that was the meaning I got out of our small chat before I dismissed him from his brilliant idea. He attempted to convince me that wasn't at all what he was implying, but I had heard all that I needed. As if I would disengage with my new play toy because he said so.

I was waiting for my brother to decide favorably on allowing Sasha and her small team to venture outside the wall. He dismissed it immediately. Not without reason but his explanations began to bore me. He was so confident in his own personal team and didn't want to offer humans any more leash then they already had. So, I offered him a week to indefinitely change his mind or I would react how I always did when I didn't get me own way. It was a threat. One that he would either take seriously because of the catastrophic result or ignore it because he thought the novelty of Sasha Pierce would soon wear off.

A loud moan pulled me out of my thoughts and back into the room. I pounded into the man from behind, my cock swelling in excitement between his cheeks and tight hole as I bit down on his neck from behind. He moaned under me, shivering as I licked over the wound and ravished his blood. I pumped again, trying to rattle off the edge that was consuming me since meeting Sasha Pierce. A woman flopped her arms over my back as she whispered sweet things. She pierced her fangs into my neck as she began fisting the other guys cock from behind. Her moans were a mere mumble echoing in the shadows of my private chambers. The human male groaned and became short of breath. I pumped into him one more time to tether him over. He blew onto the wooden floor before the fireplace, slumping forward as he whimpered in pleasure for me to stop.

I still couldn't take the edge off. They were both beautiful creatures. The man had long blonde hair cascading over his delicate shoulders and frame. The woman with short black hair had tan skin that shimmered in the day. Her kinky side was as filthy as her mouth. Such an interesting combo would usually please me and yet I felt even more on edge as I discovered I couldn't yet be pleased.

A familiar array of steel and floral combined swept underneath my nose. I pulled out of the man who slumped further into the wooden floors. The woman dropped to her knees and began to suck me off, her tongue bar rubbing back and forth under the length of my cock.

My cock itched in her mouth but not because of her talented tongue but because of that all-consuming scent that was within the castle. I pushed the woman's head back and looked at the two parties of entertainment in the past two hours. "Continue pleasing one another," I simply said and left the room. I flashed through my private chambers and into the audience room within the castle. I busted open the large wooden doors into the throne room. My entrance ignited an echo as I broke into the room.

There stood my Darling Sasha, having an audience with my brother who sat on his throne. She looked over her shoulder. Her eyes raked down my stomach and onto my all-consuming cock. Her eyes fixated and dilated for a moment. Her breath hitched and her heartbeat accelerated. She looked away. I stood there smug and proud. I knew I had a body that all desired. Not even my little mouse could ignore its beauty.

"Where are your clothes Kyran?" My brother said, positioned on his throne beyond her. It wasn't the first time he was bearing witness to my God given body. I waltzed up to where she stood. I began wiping away the blood that was smeared on my neck. The puncture wounds had healed but the traces of blood were still present. I stood next to her, indulging in her overpowering scent. There was no way that my cock would go down while she was standing in the same room. All I wanted to do was the exact same fucking I'd been doing only minutes ago but with her instead.

"Why are you having an audience with Sasha?" I asked. My brother raised his eyebrows at me. If he wanted a challenge, I would grant it to him. I brooded for a moment before Galador, who stood behind him, intervened. The few guards that were in the room kept their gaze forward.

"We have a few questions for Miss Pierce. Need you be reminded that she is not yours," Galador said quietly under his breath so only I could hear. A very daring statement for the man that was nothing more than a butler and I could kill in a second if I had to reinforce my point. I had killed my father after all. A butler would be less.

"She is mine," I said blatantly and disregarding anything else he had to say.

"I'm not yours," she said angrily. Instead of meeting my gaze, her eyes dropped to my cock and back to my brother.

"Don't look at my brother when your body is reacting to mine, little mouse," I said.

"Kyran, either leave or stand to the side," my brother said measuring me equally. How would I react, that was his question? My brother was as calculating as always. When you lived with someone for so many hundreds of years their patterns became intangible.

"I'm fine," Sasha cussed me under her breath. I continued to stare at my brother, infuriated that he called upon an audience with what I had already so boldly claimed as my plaything. Surely he wasn't interested in her as well. I snarled and decided to take a few steps to the side. I leaned up against the wall closely positioned beside one of the guards. I felt his eyes peering down on my cock every so often. After an uncomfortable silence thanks to my brothers and Galador's boring presence, they continued.

"I haven't had any reports from your father for eight days now," my brother announced as way of interrogation. "Instead, I've received forged written notes from you. No one on the wall has seen him during that period either. It was only six days ago that you requested to go beyond the walls with your own cultivated team. Care to explain?"

Sasha didn't flinch under the steely gaze of my brother or shift uncomfortably because of my broody stare. I crossed my arms, comforting myself for the answer. She had been silent about her father for the most part. Her shoulders dropped as if she had been caught out.

"My Father went beyond the wall. When he didn't return after two days, I wanted to go out and find him discreetly. I don't know how he passed through the wall so I could only consider getting through the gates by way of permission from the throne."

My brother tapped his finger a few times in thought. His suspense threshold always outweighed mine. I could see his mind ticking over as he considered the plausible outcomes. "You understand it's a punishable crime by not reporting this to me immediately."

"I am aware," she said in the same tone. He considered that as well.

"Why would your father seek to go outside the wall? Is he offering intelligence to another Kingdom?" he asked under scrutiny.

"No!" She discouraged. Her tone mixed with desperation, a quiver that I never thought would be in her character. She stepped back into herself. "My father is loyal."

"So why the sudden disappearance?" He asked. Galador's eyes were just as icy. He looked at her, displeased. He hadn't liked her from the moment I first took interest in her, but to now have not only my attention but my brother's as well must have been driving him insane. Galador was predictable. She was a problem in his eyes.

"Because he believes my mother is alive," she said depleted. My brother's eyebrows shot up as he rested his finger on his lip in consideration.

"On what basis would he believe this?" He asked. An interesting development if her crazy scientist mother is still alive. How had she lasted all this time? It was still an act of treason on his behalf even if he did chase after her. I rolled my eyes. Humans and their emotions.

"He told me that he had seen her beyond the wall one-night waving for him to go over," she said uncomfortably. "He began to act strange the following days and wanted me to go with him. I thought he was ill and going delusional. I forced him to rest and took his shift that day. When I went back to his home, he was gone. No one on the wall saw how he left and I haven't been able to find him within the city."

After much consideration my brother stood up and reflected on his throne. "Guards!" They reacted as quickly as he spouted his commandment to charge her.

I stood in front of her with lightning speed. "No one is touching what is mine," I growled at my brother. He pulled back his lips slightly to bare his fangs. I reciprocated the gesture.

"Kyran, as much as I am delighted that you've found a play toy, until this investigation is over, she will remain-"

"With me," I concluded. "And if you decided otherwise then I will so kindly burn everyone within this city to the ground," I said with a crazed chuckle. "And I'll enjoy it."

Sasha attempted to change my mind but I ignored her. I wouldn't let my brother take what was mine. Galador hadn't the balls to intervene between Amell and me. Physically I could take him, and I would dick slap his face at the end just to mortify him further. My brother growled and stared; I could see his mind ticking over in calculation. Like always he thought out his next step until his shoulders deflated slightly.

"Don't lose sight of how serious a matter this is," Amell said permitting me my way.

"I've always taken every order you've given me very seriously brother," I said acting wounded by his words.

"Amell…" Galador began in disagreement. Amell raised his hand and I smiled at Galador who too often spoke out of order.

"While we're all in the same room," I began. "I considered that this might be good timing to raise the question of my serious request. Perhaps gathering a small little human group to go beyond the walls and search for Paps ought to do the trick."

"That's irrelevant now!" Amell said infuriated. "Can't you see we have a bigger issue at hand! For all we know her father is a spy. Or her crazed mother is alive and still crafting weapons we will never understand!" He said this pointedly at Sasha who didn't move. Her heart skipped a beat. He saw her as a failed experiment and one that he would have to monitor closely because of her parents' unknown motives.

"You know I take these things very seriously brother. But furthermore, I keep to my word," I said offering him one more chance. He was to give me permission or I would do whatever I wanted anyway.

"Just for once Kyran, listen to your King," my brother seethed begrudgingly.

"My King?" I said in curious wonder. The last King that sat on the throne, I had killed with my bare hands. And that was my father. Though I didn't want to kill my brother, his tone urged me to do something a little bit more dramatic in repute.

"Kyran," Sasha said again interrupting my dark thoughts that swirled around me like a charming song. And again, I would allow myself to be swept away with it. She placed her hand on my lower back to grab my attention. "Kyran, we need to leave," she said in a tone that was small in comparison to her usual strong and steely one.

I had been permitted to monitor her personally instead of seeing her chained in a cell. But that just wasn't enough for me. She wanted a small team out beyond the walls and that was a silent promise I had made to her upon our first meeting. And for whatever reason, I wanted to keep a promise at least once in the entirety of my life. I would make that dire wish come true for my little pet human. But furthermore, I was curious as to how much I could push my brother. Would he continue to say no to me? Did he forget that although he might be King, I wasn't to ever be denied?

"Okay," I said and looked over my shoulder to Amell and Galador who were cautious of my next actions. *Okay brother. Let my next play be tremendous.*

CHAPTER
7

A MUSICAL CHARM AND A SLAUGHTERHOUSE

"SASHA, DARLING, BRING EVERY WEAPON you think you'd need to fight an army of vampires," I said as I waited outside her window. The manufactured moonlight sprawled over me. I had waited for sundown before I disturbed her. I had given her a few private hours after escorting her home. I considered it a generous amount of time before I dragged her along and into my master plan. I had been waiting patiently perched on top of the church until the sun went down.

She crept from the shadows of her room, where only candlelight fluttered behind her. She peered outside her window, infuriated by my presence as always. She closed her eyes, sighed, and pinched her nose. "What are you up to this time?" She asked gritting her teeth. I charmed a smile in response. Perhaps she was coming around to my wicked ways.

"You want to kill all the big bad vampires, don't you? Let's start with something small. I think it'll be a fun date," I added with excitement. I usually executed these magnificent spectacles on my own. I was invigorated at the thought of having a partner in crime that might just lose to their inner monster as much as me. I was giddy at the thought. I anticipated the theatrical dance of the massacre to come.

She sighed in defeat. "You know that whatever you are planning will only make my situation worse with the King. Somewhere in that crazy mind of yours you do understand that, don't you?" I looked up at her wide eyed. That was obvious and it still didn't affect my decision. My plan wouldn't be changed. This would be *fun*.

Amell was being a bore, yet again. His personality lacked in vitality. One of us had to be fun. He had too many rules and regulations, restraining my ability to be the monster that I was. *That we all were*. This was nothing more than an outburst of being told 'no,' like all the other ones I had in the past.

He always sat, poised on his throne, considering the most cautious and reasonable step. In contrast, I took immediate action and would kill the masses of those who stood in our way. The most effective and devastating tactic was to always do the unexpected, then our enemies would never have time to prepare. No one could ever counter unpredictability. And that was me—the wild card.

He was lucky to have a brother like me who was such a willing participant. So now I had to force his hand to move. He danced around the edges of this coming war for far too long and amongst it found time to threaten to take away my personal toy and entertainment. Now I would make sure he focused on his own problems.

He won't have time to focus on what my darling Sasha and I are up to. I would be able to have a fun bloodbath tonight and receive my happily ever after once I'm done.

"We're going to start a war," I whispered in excitement. "I'll give you two minutes. If you're not ready by then I will leave without you. Though, you might find yourself in a cellar if you're not strapped to my side–Kings orders." I chimed with a brazen smile.

With an ungrateful growl, Sasha pulled back into the shadows of her apartment. I was curious as to what her apartment looked like inside. I imagined that she was a minimalist, living amongst the few things that she needed to survive with few luxuries.

I could sense that I was being watched. From the moment we stepped out of the castle grounds I was followed. They weren't close enough to hear me, they wouldn't dare venture so close. I already anticipated that when we made a run for the gates, I'd have to dispose of them before they informed Amell. I didn't care if they were my brother's personal spies. All was fair in the games of war.

I could hear Sasha shuffling through weapons. I had been confident that she would join. She didn't really have an option. Fight by my side or be dragged to a cellar to be left alone. Despite her peculiar ability, I would kill majority of the vampires tonight with speed she'd never witnessed before. Simply, I want to impress her. She would see how powerful I was firsthand and succumb to the desire of wanting to touch, pet, and play with me. It was inevitable.

She would be capable of handling herself amongst the few vampires that might remain. It piqued my interest as to how many vampires she could handle before being overwhelmed. I never considered that I would think of a human to be as monstrous a fighter as a well-aged vampire.

I wondered if she would recede into herself once overrun or transcend into something more formidable. Fight or flight. Instinct to survive was what triggered any living creature's most barbaric nature. I couldn't wait to see Sasha's most beautiful form. I wanted to see the extremes of what her mother had crafted from her daughter's living body. How far could this one tiny human go before imploding from that curse of hers?

Or consequently she might break. I doubted she'd fought so many vampires at once. Perhaps she wasn't the fighter I considered her to be. If that came to be, then I suppose my play toy was broken and there was no point in keeping her around.

She clocked in the security code to her apartment door as she left. She was strapped in tight leather that so sweetly kissed her inner thighs. It wasn't the heavy armor that I expected her to wear. Her choice of clothing was light and durable so she could move swiftly through the masses. Risky considering her flesh was so thin and her body fragile. Nonetheless, I admired the attire. She looked like a death god as she strapped another dagger around her inner thigh. The weight of her weapons alone indicated she had more strength and balance than an average human. Otherwise, she wouldn't be able to walk so boldly with so many jingling at her side. She was designed to unsheathe so many weapons and to kill on demand. She was utterly ravishing.

"Stop looking at me like that and focus on this stupid war you want to start," she said in a steely tone. She looked around to see if we were being watched. No one crept out of their hiding. We hadn't moved yet. But when we would, they would chase, fast. And I was prepared for that. I was excited by the thought.

"It's hard for me to decide if I'd rather stay a night in to fuck you or slaughter unsuspecting victims in the night. I've never been so torn before," I said earnestly. The way her inner thighs brushed past one another as she walked had me leaning towards her in anticipation. Within seconds, she grabbed the dagger from the side of her leg and threw it at me. I cackled catching it before it hit its target and went through my skull. Maybe she would be keen for the fucking next time. I admired her dagger that had been beautifully carved. Before I could admire the inscription and heavy weight further, she took it from my hand and sheathed it once again. I sighed in admiration for this brutal woman. She knew how to make me tick. I focused on the task at hand. *Think about fucking her later, okay?* I internally slapped myself.

"So, everything that is about to unfold will happen very quickly, okay?" I said. She sighed and shook her head.

"You're not the first male to say that to me." I blinked a few times, utterly shocked that my little mouse had made a joke. I cackled absolutely delighted that she could manifest a joke from her bitter soul. She cringed at my laugh, evidently regretting having made the joke. "I can't believe I'm actually going along with this," she said, rubbing her forehead and shaking her head from side to side. She took one final breath and then her iron persona took over. Sasha was now ready to hunt. "Let's just get this over with. I'm ready," she breathed.

"Fabulous," I purred. "Don't scream." I grabbed under her thighs and held her close to my chest. With the speed that I grabbed her she hmphed. It was an acknowledgment on her behalf that I was faster piggybacking her than we would be running together. She clasped her hands around my neck. Not that she needed such security, I could hold her light weight forever without ever being tired.

I ran for the wall, arriving within seconds. I placed Sasha gently against the wall behind me and grabbed the first vampire by the neck who heeded chase. There were eight of them, easy pickings. All of them clattered in their weak armor that would do nothing to stop me. I smiled and ripped the head off from the first vampire I had so easily grabbed. His body began to decay immediately. This would be quick. The rest seemed startled. Did they actually consider they might be a challenge for me?

One went to make a break for it and run back towards the castle to report to my brother. I stood in front of her path with lightning speed. "Hello, Darling," I said, and punctured my nails into her chest cavity and ripped out her heart. The others ambushed with unison and ability of phenomenal training. Yet, if my brother had been serious, he should've come himself with an army. I backhanded one across the face with such force that he splattered against the wall. Sasha jumped on him and plunged one of her swords through his chest. Well at least I wouldn't have to bother with that one anymore.

Two circled me and jumped. One went high and one went low. I stepped back yawning at the maneuver. What a boring technique. One of their swords glided towards where my ankles had been. I jumped on his blade and balanced on top of it in theatrical pause. I looked down on him. The horror on his face in that moment meant everything to me. I had the moon shining down from behind me, cascading the gleam of death in my eye. Today I was his reaper. As the second vampire tried to pierce my chest with his sword, I grabbed it, my blood splattering everywhere as the blade sliced into my hand. I clutched it halfway down the blade. I palmed his elbow snapping bone in half and shredding it entirely off. I grabbed the handle of the sword that still had his dangling arm and decapitated the vampire beneath me.

His sword dipped as his body began to decay. I decapitated the second vampire's head, swinging beautifully in full circle. The other two vampires had turned to report to the castle. I steadied for only a moment before harpooning the blade through the back of one of the vampires and striking his heart. He plummeted in a decaying mass.

Before I could run for the remaining vampire a dagger blazed past my face and struck home into the back of the last survivor. Sasha had hit her mark just as I had. Buildings away and she had hit her target. The vampire slumped into a mass of decay. Well, maybe even for a human she would keep up.

No vampire survived which meant there were none to report to my brother. I collected Sasha in my arms once again and ran along the wall with splendid speed. I wasn't stupid enough to take them to the spot where we snuck out every night. When I did find our foxhole, I jumped up and through it. The soldiers on duty pretended to have not seen anything. They were either ignorant or perhaps didn't see us at such speed. Perhaps they had a keen eye like Sasha as well if they had been experimented on by Sasha's mother.

Beyond the walls, the breeze howled from the cold of night. It was nearing midnight as I passed through the mass of terrain for an hour. Tonight would even tire me slightly. I looked forward to my well-deserved sleep that was to come. The terrain drifted from its mountains and forestry that attempted to thrive and turned to dirt. Oppollo's region wasn't as beautiful as ours. It was barren, dry, and coarse much like the ruling of its King. I wouldn't go for King Oppollo directly tonight. No, I had in mind a small village that his new soldiers trained at.

I was curious as to how quickly he would retaliate after I destroyed his unsuspecting soon to be warriors. Would he offer my brother days or only hours of silence? Or would he succumb to waving a white flag? That much I highly doubted. If I went straight for King Oppollo then I would solve my brother's problem for him. This way, my boring brother would have to prepare for a retaliation, and I could go about my daily business without such a watchful eye.

I had only met Oppollo once during my Father's rein. I measured in that one meeting that he was a hard man and blood thirsty vampire. I was surprised he hadn't acted for domination sooner. I trusted my abilities to kill but also understood caution, if ever necessary. He had been the only vampire I'd met that instinctually triggered such a dangerous alarm. So instead of facing him head on and gamble with my own life, I decided it would be fun to provoke him from the side and let my brother deal with the consequence. That would keep Amell's focus off my little mouse for some time.

The howl of the wind brushed past us. I tried my hardest to cover Sasha with my arms as much as possible. The last thing I wanted was for her limbs to be frozen as I dropped her in the middle of a battlefield. We were approaching the village and as expected, they were unsuspecting of my arrival. Large towering flames burnt in the distance so they could see through the night. They weren't as technologically focused as us and they trained their warriors in a very primal way. I found Oppollo's people primitive all together.

They slept underground in bunkers during the day to avoid the sun. The humans managed throughout the day harvesting their own means to survive. I targeted this village purposefully because of its representation. Oppollo's upcoming warriors all gone in the blink of a night. It only contained a few hundred with a mixture of both humans and vampires. I had no issue with killing the humans as well if they were to get in my way. I was excited by the few high-ranking warriors that were in this camp who trained them. At least they would offer a challenge.

As we darted closer to the outskirts, I quickly calculated

the most flamboyant entrance. The bell had begun to ring in alarm as we made our entrance. I jumped towards one of the open barrel flames tipping it towards the ground over the wall. I skidded on the wall kicking over a barrel of oil as they combined and went up in flames against the wall. I jumped off, avoiding the combustion. The flames began to viciously lick at a wooden building close by and screams began to erupt. The first flame began to spread the fire amongst the masses of buildings that were to burn tonight.

In the center of the village, I elegantly placed Sasha's tip toes on the ground to make sure after the speed that which we ran, she could still stand. She was as resilient as I anticipated. Her swords glided out from the sheaths in her back as she axed away at an arrow that shot for us. I looked up into the direction at the first barrage of vampires that would come to attack. Despite our lack of welcoming, all I could think as I saw the muscle in her arms flex to cut away oncoming arrows was: *'I love you.'* The jagged scar that ran down her neck in a ruthless way shone in the moonlight and flames that were blazing. Her eyes were focused, and her breathing was short. Every muscle was lean and ready for battle. My human battle goddess. My fixation was tempting in dangerous territory as I considered a word I had never used in my life. *Love.* This ravishing woman had to be mine in every way. *If* she were to survive the night.

CHAPTER
8

SCREAMS TO MY BLEEDING EARS

THE HUMANS SCREAMED AND RAN towards the back of the village as the vampires silently paraded towards us. They circled us, outnumbering us vastly. Smoke billowed into the night sky as the village caught alight from the one barrel of oil and open fire I kicked over upon entering. I smiled in glee. What a disastrous vision in all its glory and I was in the center of it all.

A bell rang in the distance to alarm all soldiers that me, myself, and I, was here—oh, and Sasha as well of course. She held steady preparing for the vampires to make the first move but the showman in me wanted to peacock how amazing I truly was. I planned to kill majority of them before she even delighted in the taste. I wanted to tease her in foreplay without offering her the real bite. Her pupils began to dilate in and out, threatening to dissolve into all black. A sign and trigger that she would surely lose control.

My little mutated human had already tapped into the hatred she felt towards my species. *She was utterly sensational and a beauty in all her glory.*

Disappointed that no one offered a personal invite to die first, I blasted through the first row with a vengeance. I swiftly rifled through the masses avoiding their obvious attacks and began extracting hearts and decapitating them one by one with a wicked smile. I bit down on my lips reveling in the taste of my own blood as I swept through them with something that transcended arousal. This was my very essence at its core being set free. I was on fire with everything else around me and free to dance to the tune that was a constant echo in my head. Hickory, Dickory, Dock.

Swords, nails, and teeth came at me. So primitive and predictable. I dodged them with ease wondering if this was their first day of training. So sloppy. Perhaps this would be over a lot sooner than I anticipated. A gun shot went off and the bullet darted towards me. I stepped to the side, to dodge it by inches. The bullet broke into tiny fragments and tiny bits of silver punctured all down my left side. My entire left side was riddled in fragments of silver. Each individual wound felt like it was set alight as my body tried to push out the foreign object that offered me such pain. Pleasurable. It reminded me that even I too could bleed like a broken man.

Another two gunshots went off. I couldn't move fast enough to avoid the bullets as my left side staggered its pace. Now this was slightly more exciting. I grabbed one of the vampires nearby with my right arm and used him as a shield. The swell of pain was phenomenal as my blood attempted to push the fragments out before my body regenerated with them still inside. *Mother fuckers found a new gun, how lovely.*

A vampire from behind jumped above me to slice his sword through me. I quickly considered my options. I could shift slightly but probably have my left arm amputated. It would regenerate but would take a few hours which didn't help me now. My second option was to shift in the other direction but would have to take another bitchy silver bullet. And this time it might even hit my face. *Goodbye left arm, you have to go!* I anticipated the sharp blade to slice through, angling myself enough so I could go for his throat afterwards.

The animalistic growl that came from Sasha was intoxicating. She deflected the sword and slashed at his face. The vampire howled and clutched at his face. My arm was still entirely intact. She hoisted me under my shoulder and jumped us out of the way from the barrage of dispersing silver bullets.

She found cover behind one of the burning buildings, resting me on a beam that had not yet gone ablaze. My body began to push out the tiny scraps of silver. Painful bastards. They tinkled on the ground, piece by piece. The sound was like a rainfall of shrapnel, glittering amongst the thriving flames.

Her eyes were totally enveloped in black and then the strangest of things happened. She smiled. Like the little monster she was. She actually dared to smile and mock the very monster that I had always been. She had just saved my ass and her inner monster found that hilarious.

She confronted the vampires that came around the corner of the building, striking them down one by one in powerful sweeps. Be damned that I would let her hold saving the amputation of my left arm over me. I had been caught off guard by their new guns but wouldn't make that mistake twice. The whole ordeal had been momentarily thrilling. I swept around her with monstrous speed that she could never match. I wiped out the three vampires that she had prepared to take on. I smiled cockily over my shoulder. Sasha's nostrils flared as a low snarl came deep from her belly. She was not at all pleased that I had taken her kill. Another gunshot went off. And like a puff of smoke I was gone and in front of the very fucker that had shot me last time.

Bang. The second one went off, but my hand was already directing the gun towards the night sky. The vampire's fangs were larger than most of those around us. His uniform indicated that he was one of the instructors who had real warfare experience. I wanted to embarrass him in the greatest possible way. I dove my fangs into his neck, ripping savagely into him. His gurgling roar satisfied me as he clawed at my face trying to push me off. He tasted like utter garbage. I ripped out the side of his throat and upper cut my fist through his rib cage and held firm onto his heart.

"Those nasty bullets hurt," I said to him and ripped out his dead heart. I pitched his heart at an oncoming vampire. It slapped onto his face and I laughed. Waves of vampires swept in and encompassed us. I killed some efficiently and others comically, smiling like the devil I was.

"Kyran!" I recognized the voice and turned to face the man who dared to interrupt my fun. I tore apart the small vampire in my hands. Limb from limb. He had the audacity to latch onto my arm. Ghastly little thing. I placed my hand oh so gently in his mouth and broke his skull apart, ripping the top of his face off from the hinges of his jaw. I stared down the vampire who had shouted out my name the entire time. I remembered him. He was one of Oppollo's finest warriors and overseer. He had been introduced to my father as well. *What was his name again?* "We had a treaty!" He seethed "What is this?"

The vampire that I held from the hinges of his jaw, gargled with his faceless body dangling in my hand. I looked between the bloody pile in my hands and looked back at the vampires whose name I didn't care to remember. "I call this self-explanatory." I said discarding the hideous vampire that was marring my hand with black blood. "I thought it couldn't be any clearer than this." His fellow vampires stopped momentarily, waiting for his signal. I circled, pointing at the decaying bodies around me. Were these not his students he was so proud of? "I mean... unless you need me to spell it out for you?"

Sasha skidded to my side, dirt flicking up in her wake. She was ravished to kill more. Her face was slick with black blood. She had a few cuts, scratches, and bite marks. I could see black venom oozing from where she had been bitten. Filthy mutts had tried to paralyze her by injecting their venom. I was enraged that the filthy mutts had the audacity to taste what was mine.

She was eyeing the overseer in center of their formation. "No. The big one's mine," I said chastising her. She growled at me in response. I didn't even know if my Darling Sasha was of human mind right now. "Now," I said to the good for nothing overseer who liked to talk too much, well aware that I had done most of the talking. I charmed an elegant smile. "I'm wanting to get this over and done with before dinner, so if we could carry on, that'd be swell."

A creak from beneath us sounded before I could sense the movement. I grabbed Sasha under the legs and jumped high and out of the way from the silver trap that snapped shut beneath us. Hundreds of tiny thin teeth snapped shut on thin air. *Well that could've been delightfully messy.* A silver net shot at us from the guard wall as we suspended in the air. I twisted sharply to avoid its harpooning speed and dove my hand into the brick of one of the buildings. We drifted down only inches and hung on the side of the building. Gun fires shot in our direction. I released my hand, so we dropped towards the ground. Sasha kicked against the building, shifting our position to avoid two bullets that began to splinter into silver shrapnel. Only a few pieces punctured into my arm but not enough to affect my mobility like last time. *Her senses were keen. We danced in perfect harmony on the battlefield.* I was right to bring her along with me for fun. Her mother certainly wasn't lacking in vision when it came to experiment on her own daughter.

I let Sasha down gently as our feet touched the ground. There must've only been fifty vampires left. They had tried to rely on their machinery and failed. I didn't want to stretch this out for much longer. I wasn't thrilled by the idea of having to hide outside the wall if the sun reached us before we made it back to Grand Klaus. It was time to finalize this very clear message.

Humans huddled in the corner of the village screaming. A few vampires stood in front of them as if to protect them. I'd make sure to kill them before we left and leave the humans to remain shaking in their inability to protect themselves.

Some humans had been caught in the crossfire. Some had even attempted to fight alongside their masters. Human blood and vampire decay mixed with the aroma of billowing smoke. The entire village would soon entirely burn to the ground. It was time to end this game.

I locked eyes with their overseer and ran at him. His remaining soldiers rallied and split separate ways. If any of them got in my way, I disposed of them quickly. This was only his and my grand theatrical stage now. I wanted to spike him in the center of this village still gaping and bleeding out alive. By the time King Oppollo arrived, his overseer would be gasping for forgiveness and unable to unhinge himself.

Respectively, instead of using any weapons he approached me using himself as the tool. I could appreciate a fellow vampire who believed in the monster that he was instead of the weapons that came from the humans' original knowledge. I punched at him and he dodged. He kicked at me and I avoided it. We were simply toying with one another and testing each other out.

He snarled and lunged into a full tackle, a very confronting maneuver but one that I appreciated. He evidently didn't want to play games for too long. He was as boring as his King. He lifted me up and slammed me through the bricks of a burning building. We smashed amongst the billowing smoke. Neither of us were affected by the black smoke or inability to see. I pushed back his shoulders with force. His nails scraped along my back and across my ribs before taking sturdy steps back. *Oh, how I was aroused by the smell of my own blood during a fight.* Hickory, Dickory, Dock.

I charmed a smile letting him bear witness to the fangs and malicious face that would be his demise. Whether he seriously thought he could take me on or not was irrelevant. This would end the same even despite his optimism. Sasha guarded the building we had broken into. She fought off vampires who tried to enter and help their leader. She wouldn't let anyone interfere with my victory.

He lunged for me again. I blocked his sharp nails that dove for my chest. He kicked at my leg but I avoided it by stepping back. It didn't take me long to assess his form and pivots. When he struck again, I purposefully stepped into the punch that punctured my collarbone. His nails clutched at the bone and shattered it to pieces. I didn't balk or cry like he might've anticipated. He had been aiming for my heart after all.

I held onto his arm that was still penetrating my collarbone. I slashed across his face. His hand blocked majority of the strike. My nails were still in reach to puncture and rip out one of his eyes. He squirmed only for a second still trying to take his hand out of my shoulder. I held onto his arm firmly so he had no such luxury. I would not return that hand. I placed my foot behind him and pushed him over. He kicked his legs into my stomach in attempt to roll me over. I held my grip on his arm that was still interlocked with my collar. His nails twisted. My bones shattered and squirmed as it began to distort. The pain was a pleasure.

I pressed my knee to his face to keep him down before he could get back up. His arm was oddly jarred as I kept it pinned within me. I twisted his arm, snapping it in half but not enough to tear it off. He grunted and tried to swing his legs back up. I headbutted his knees to block him from swinging over and back onto his feet. My head split open and began to bleed out, immediately dripping down my face and chin. I looked over him with a smile.

"You're a failure," I said and plunged my hand towards his throat. He grabbed my wrist and with all his might pulled away from its grasp. My smile widened as the blood from my forehead began to drip onto his face. Inch by inch I continued to apply the pressure and grasp my nails into his throat. My nails dug in with uncontrollable excitement. No one could match me on strength. I was a monster unleashed. I continued to press down as he tried to take his arm out of my collar but I held his grip firm. He had nowhere to go. My collarbone was shattered. But that was irrelevant. I had already won. Every other part of him bucked and clawed at me, ripping apart bits of my body that I could dispose of. I wasn't the one about to eternally die.

With one final push of pressure, I crumbled my hand through his throat and the back of his neck. Pop. His head split across the room and into the billowing smoke. His body went limp around me. I looked down at his decaying hand that was twisted in my collarbone. "Ewww," I said detaching it. "I didn't put much thought into that," I considered. Ew, Ew, Ew. Dead man's hand in my shoulder. I was disappointed that I didn't stick to my original theatrical plan to prop him on a stick in the village center but was satisfied with the end result.

I wiped over my shoulder defiantly wanting to scrub out the filth of his touch. *Gross. Dead man hand in my body.* Sasha let loose a gurgling scream. My body reacted before I had time to think. I ripped apart the two vampires who had pinned her against the wall and bitten into her. The next few moments were a blur of blood spluttering everywhere. She did well to hold them off for so long. But she was only one human after all. No matter how exceptional.

I came to her aid assessing the puncture marks. They had torn rather viciously at her throat and chest. "It's okay," I said. She tried to steady her breathing but was coughing from the inhalation of smoke.

"I know," she said through a rasp and pressed off the building, clutching at her wound. Her eyes were still enveloped in black as she searched through the graveyard to see if there were any survivors. She was still on the hunt. She took a step towards the humans and I intervened. Not that I cared for the humans. But I imagined that her more rational and human conscious did.

"Sasha," I said collecting her face into my hands. She looked over my shoulder at the huddled and scared villagers. She didn't even flinch away from my touch. "They're human." She snarled in response. I firmly held her face so she couldn't look away from me nor prey on the humans further. She sneered at me in response. "Pull your bitchy attitude in," I said. I was conflicted. It turned me on as much as it ached me to see. She was going against the very nature she believed in. But this darkness of hers intrigued me beyond measure. I so badly wanted to consume it myself.

She snarled at me again her grip now coming around my wrists and her blunt nails digging in. I could see the reflection of myself in those heavenly black enveloped eyes. A monster reflecting a monster. But past that was the first woman who had ever ventured on a massacre with me and she was only human. *I* was the one pulling *her* back.

The stench of her foreign blood burned my nostrils. I was aroused by this demon that was summoned to my side. Fate had brought her into my path to toy with. Damned if I do and damned if I don't. I pressed my lips closer to hers. My body reacted on its own, taking what it had craved for so long now. Her hot breath flushed through me. My body didn't need such things as breath but consuming hers made me feel *alive*. Her upper lip brushed past mine and she nipped at me. I was startled if anything. I had been so transfixed in her eyes that I hadn't even realized she had bitten my lip.

"We don't bite the hand that feeds us," I chastised her. The nibble alone had my entire body in flames. My cock hardened at the conquest. Of both our enemy camp being perished and this wickedly delicious woman in front of me who dared to bite.

"You don't feed me," she snarled and tried to pull away to look over my shoulder and at the humans. I still held her face firmly so she couldn't look at anything but me.

"Oh, but how I could," I said taking her lips for myself. There was a salty mix of blood and sweat. I could taste the taint of hatred and passion for the fight. It rolled into me as I pushed against her tongue trying to make more room for my wicked ways.

I pushed against her; my cock now hard at the prospect of this monster finally submitting to me. She rolled her hips against me, moaning with the same sweet contentment. The building beside us collapsed as the flames continued to tear down the village behind us.

She pulled back with relentless force. Her eyes were no longer dilated as she stared at me with steely brown pupils. I released her. I was going against my very nature to accommodate for a human! I took what I wanted when I wanted. She took a shaky breath and pulled back her hand from the wound on her neck to see the blood. She looked around us, confused. Did she not recall any of it?

She looked past my shoulder at the whimpering humans and then back at her bloody hands. Her heart continued to thrum loudly as I felt the tension in her body rise. "It's time for us to go," she said and began walking into the direction of which we came. Her walk was strong, but I noticed the strain it was putting on her body. She didn't heal as quickly as us vampires. "We've done what you came for."

"Is that it?" I said with my cock still rock hard. Every urge in my body wanted to lunge at her and claim what was mine. It was my right and yet her one effective look kept me in my place.

"We've done enough tonight," she said and turned her back on me once again. I moved my dick uncomfortably. I could feel the passion running through her only seconds ago. Her touch reacted to mine. Her body thrummed to be wrapped around mine and heaving to have my cock inside of her. Was it possible that I had met someone even more messed up then me?

"What Darling Sasha wants, Sasha gets," I chimed in a childish tone. I wanted to take her as mine right now. But a part of me wanted to continue playing this game that she now entertained. Her most primal instinct was to touch and fuck me. I would bring that out in the real Sasha, the less demon-eyed version of herself. I found both sides of her equally pleasing. I would make her submit. Hickory, dickory, dock.

CHAPTER
9

WHEN THE FOX RATTLED THE CHICKEN COOP

HAD MY BROTHER KNOWN MY clever ways of escaping the wall of Grand Klaus, I imagined I would've had a welcoming committee sooner. Instead, a few vampire guards were aimlessly searching for us outside the walls and even more throughout the city. I swept past them undetected with ease. I jumped back through our open panel that no one had yet come across. That was fault on my brother for building such a big wall. The moment someone escaped, they had no idea where to begin searching for the tiny little hole.

"Take me home," Sasha had said on more than one occasion. I ignored her. After our act of defiance against my brother, she was best kept by my side hidden in my private chambers where no one would dare venture. My wounds had already healed as expected. Sasha's however was very slowly knitting together. Despite insisting that she healed faster than other humans, it wasn't fast enough for me. I offered her some of my blood to help the healing process, but she immediately refused it. I could force it down her throat, but I anticipated she wouldn't talk to me for days. The array and temptation of her blood was pushing me over the edge. If I hadn't had years of learning to curve my appetite when necessary, she would've been ravished already.

For now, her wounds had begun to clot and I doubted at the current rate it'd take her a few days to heal. She was limp in my arms on the way back, exhausted from the fight. As expected, it was a novelty to have a pet to take care of. She was so fragile yet fierce at the same time. I believed in her ability to fight but knew that she still needed my protection. Never did I consider protecting something or someone other than myself. I'd rather kill the thing that would jeopardize my thought process in such a way. And yet as I held her tightly, I never wanted to let my possession go.

I dashed through the city and then onto the castle grounds. Guards had noticed my arrival and I knew it was only a short matter of time before my brother would be banging on my door. As soon as we reached my private living quarters, I sat Sasha gently down on the wooden armchair in my bathroom. It was glorious in size. A large inground bathtub occupied the center. Gold trimmings lavished the ceiling and floor edges. The entire room was encircled by glass windows, so I had a view of the gardens and natural river that passed through Grand Klaus. I did not shy away when the old woman who managed the gardens saw me naked on regular occasion. Or when she saw me fucking violently against the glass windows.

"Let's wash up before our guests arrive," I said

suggesting the empty bath. She scoffed at my proposition and I laughed.

"As if they would have any doubt it was you. You're just trying to mock your brother's intelligence now," she chastised. "I need to go back to my apartment."

I began stripping off my clothes and walked over to the shower in the corner of the room. Dry blood stained the entirety of my body. It was rarer to find the pale of my skin amongst the black blood that colored me.

"Do you mind?" She said looking in the other direction as I proudly passed her.

"It's nothing you haven't seen before, Sasha Darling," I said. I began to wash myself under the scalding hot water. It was a refreshing sensation after my victory. I wanted to look squeaky clean before my brother arrived so I could pretend to be innocent. I would mock my brother to only antagonize the situation further. After a few minutes I could smell him before he had reached the entrance to my abode. "Stay in here," I said to Sasha.

I clicked the door behind me and locked her in from the outside. She seethed my name inside. I charmed a smile at my little bird I'd now caged. I put on some loose fitted pants and opened the door before my brother burst in. He slammed me up against the wall, his fists pinning my shoulders. "WHAT HAVE YOU DONE?!" He growled. I knitted my eyebrows in confusion.

"Whatever do you mean?" I replied with innocent expression. He slammed me hard again. I placed my hand on his. "I would be careful if you are thinking of trying that a third time, brother. If I recall correctly, it was always you who ended up hurt when we were kids."

Galador was standing behind him with a few guards that were nothing but decor. His expression was filthy with intent. It was satisfying to see. *Job well done to me.* A smashing noise came from the bathroom. I sighed. I could smell my beautiful captive breaking free from the window she had just broken. *Why won't she ever do what I say?* Now I had to make this entertaining conversation quick. To piss her off, I wanted to reach her fortress of an apartment before she did. My little mouse was obsessed with her 'home.' Even she was smart enough to admit the safest place for her was by my side. She was in danger walking throughout a city of vampires with unwashed and scented blood on her. I could only beg the question as to why she was so desperate to return to her abode. It dawned on me that perhaps my little mouse had a secret that she wasn't willing to share. Maybe she was hiding something or someone.

"Okay, okay, okay," I said shrugging my brother off. Though he didn't seem to want to let go. I brushed him aside and pushed off the wall. "You weren't doing anything about Oppollo's silence on our treaty, so I acted on your behalf."

"You retaliated because I went after your dog!" He snapped. I pressed him up against the wall, my hand firm around his throat. He snarled at me, not even attempting to defend himself. My response was all he needed for an answer. He wanted to verify how much Sasha Darling had got under my skin. After the massacre, my temper hadn't yet entirely simmered. I would've brushed such a comment off in playful gesture. But now I reconsidered what it would be like to kill my only living family member. The soldiers pulled out their weapons and stood before Galador in protection. They surrounded me. I scoffed. Such imbeciles. I just wiped out a small arsenal. What would these aloof idiots do? *And these were the guards who would protect my brother, the oh so noble King.* Pathetic.

"What will you do," Galador calmly said. "Kill another

King? Your brother of all people for a defect human?" Already the smell of Sasha's floral and steely scent was vanishing in the distance. I couldn't let her run any further out of my reach.

"No, because that would be ridiculous," I said releasing my brother. "We needed to act. Oppollo will either step down or step up to the war. Enough waiting around. It was only a matter of time." I stepped back and put my hands in my loose pockets. I looked at the pathetic vampires who would dare raise a sword towards me in my own home. I would've killed them already if I hadn't wanted my white carpet to be replaced once again. I wanted it to be beautiful for when I returned Sasha to her new cage.

"That wasn't your choice to make!" My brother snarled as he paced back and forth in the room.

"But it was, Brother. We all make choices and mine was to act when you didn't. You should've acted first if you wanted a different outcome."

"You are not King!" My brother snapped. I charmed a wicked smile at his outburst. How very rare of him to lose control. His mind must've been reeling over for him to be so frazzled. What a delightful sight.

"I don't want your toy Kingdom," I scoffed. It was the last thing on my mind.

"Then what do you want, Kyran?" Galador intervened still hiding behind Amell's pointless guards. "What does a vampire who desires nothing live for?" Amell and I stared at him. Now I might not be a very sane person, but asking such a philosophical question right now, was not the time.

"Your dog continues to yap," I said to my brother ignoring Galador. "You left me no choice brother. I gave you an option and you chose wrong. You denied me. So I will deny you and your ability to avoid this war." I tapped him on the shoulder. "Let me know when Oppollo is near. I will stand by your side. Like always. Until then, I have somewhere else to be."

"Kyran!" My brother shouted at me, but I had already left the room. I stepped into the bathroom and looked at my showerhead that had been broken off the wall and used as a weapon to smash out my window. My God, she was determined to race back to her apartment. That had me curious beyond measure. I was certain that my little mouse was definitely hiding something because she wouldn't run into danger so knowingly. I caught the wave of her beautiful scent and located her in a backroad within the city. She was weak and slow. Instead of scoping her up in assistance of her fragile state, I ran past her, eager to break into her apartment before she arrived. I would find out what my little mouse was hiding. She screamed out my name as she felt the air of my existence dash past her. Let's see what trouble this little vixen was truly about.

CHAPTER 10

THE MAD SCIENTIST

W ITHIN THE PARAMETER OF HER apartment building, her security system opened fire a barrage of arrows my way. I avoided them and deflected three with ease. I jumped into her bedroom window, hiding my face from the glittering splinters of glass that shattered around me. Cuts bled and then healed within seconds. I dropped onto the floor of her room, pleased with the shards of glass shimmering on the unpolished wooden floors. An eye for an eye. It was only fair after she had broken my window to escape my bathroom. I shook my head back and forth shaking pieces out of my hair. I was excited to finally see inside the little mouse's den.

It was exactly how I had envisioned it—minimalist. There was a single bed positioned in the corner of the shoebox room. A tall ceiling sized mirror was positioned across from it. In the corner beside her bed was a wardrobe. I inspected the top drawer. All her panties were boring. No lace whatsoever. That'd be something I'd fix. I collected one of the grey boring ones and stretched it out. Not even a thong. I shook my head in disapproval and threw it over my shoulder and onto the floor. I inspected the private ensuite. It was as functional as her bedroom. It fitted with a shower, toilet, and single basin. The only add ons were a bar of soap, toilet paper, toothbrush, and toothpaste. I closed the door to the bathroom wishing I hadn't witnessed the tragic lifestyle she led. *My Sasha Darling, who swapped your home out for a prison cell?*

The entire bedroom smelled of Sasha but there was something beyond her scent that caught my interest. I walked through the door that opened into a small living room and a kitchen that was hidden by a wall in the corner. A double sofa was positioned in front of an outdated television that had begun to collect dust. The side light in the kitchen was turned on and flies collected on a sandwich she had been making before I interrupted her. She took more care of her training equipment in the abandoned pool room over her own inhabitants.

I could sense another two humans in the apartment building. I had always noticed that there were another two, of what I assumed to be tenants. Their heartbeats were erratic. Their scents made me pull back my nose in hesitation to take another whiff. I couldn't pinpoint the smell, but it repulsed me.

I could sense Sasha running closer towards her abode. Why was my little mouse monopolizing an almost abandoned building? I listened out for the erratic beating hearts and decided to follow the mystery behind them. Perhaps these humans were her hidden secret. I walked through the living room and out the front door that led onto a hallway. A small light flickered on and off in a futile attempt to remain on. The trimmings on the walls were dusty and the smell of mold overwhelmed my nose.

I looked down either side of the hallway and followed the trace of the erratic heart beats. I ventured right. What was my little mouse hiding? There was a door for an abandoned apartment on my left. On my right was the door to the pool room that she used for training. I came to a dead end and grimaced as I opened the door to the cleaning closet. I was certain this was the only way to reach the humans. Sasha was close now. I had to find whatever bizarreness she was hiding before she found me first.

The light continued to flicker on and off in the hallway behind me. I curiously looked through the cleaning cupboard, that only contained a broom and mop. Neither had been used in months. Cobwebs had begun to form on them. I listened carefully, pinpointing the exact location of the heartbeats that were underneath me. I searched the walls and ceilings to see if there was some magnificent trap door. No such thing and if there were, I simply couldn't find it. Keeping in mind that Sasha was rounding the corner to her apartment building, I shrugged my shoulder. *Well that left me no choice.* I could just break in the floorboard. I raised my leg and smashed my foot through the flooring. It obliterated and I looked down into the gloomy hole as the mop bucket bounced on the floor beneath. *If the mop bucket didn't trigger any security trap then I should be fine,* I considered. I dove through.

The room was dark and a mixture of foreign smells. My eyes adapted quickly to the dark as I circled the room with my eyes. Behind me was a door. *Well I'll be damned, there was a door after all.* There must've been a secret stairwell somewhere in the building. A leak in the roof continued to drip. It pattered every few seconds. The room smelt of stale walls and mold grew underneath the floorboards that I had just busted through. The ground was cemented and filthy with remnants of mud. It had been scraped up and swept from what looked like a flood.

I rose my eyebrows in surprise at the two vampires that were strung open along the wall. They were strapped in silver so they couldn't move. Their arms and legs were stretched out. A silver strap was burned into their neck so they couldn't move. Their neck had tried to regenerate but molded with the silver. Neither of them was conscious. Their veins were dark blue and shimmering through their porcelain and exhausted skin. For how long had they been starved?

Staged across the vampires were two cages that imprisoned humans. They were frail and malnourished. Their cages smelt of feces and urine. They shuddered in the cold and away from me, terrified. Their wrinkly and exhausted bodies struggled to breath under the density of air in the room. That explained the erratic heartbeats. It would appear my little mouse had some pets of her own. I scanned the display cabinets that showcased bottles with odd substances, titled with scribbles I'd never seen before. In the center of the room was a silver gurney with thick silver straps. Positioned beside it was a small removable silver table with sharp tools that I'd only ever seen in the use of torture. I was impressed by her selection. I opened the small drawer underneath that consisted of long needles and vials that contained colored liquids. In the corner of the room was a wooden desk. Stacks of paper with crazy scribblings were not so neatly piled on the desk.

Sasha attempted to be quiet as she walked down the steps. Never would this woman be able to sneak up on me. The wound on her neck had reopened and the erotic smell of her blood flooded into the room. She must've scurried back desperately to reopen a wound on her neck. She stood at the door and before she creaked it open, I spoke.

"Sasha Darling," I said turning around to face her. She creaked open the door and her silhouette came into focus. Those brown eyes seemed to glow in the dark. She was like a predator whose cave had been infiltrated. Despite the darkness in the room her gaze was intent on me. She could see me just as well and clearly as I saw her. This sensitive and attractive human was fully aware of the stakes right now. I had crept in and exposed her darkest secret. "Did you take up your mother's work?" I asked curiously. I approached one of the vampires causally and raised a finger to touch him.

"Don't touch him!" She outbursts. I looked back at her and growled low from the bottom of my throat. My upper lip pulled back slightly to reveal my aged fangs. I didn't like it much when she defended another male, no matter the circumstance. If she had said '*it,*' I would've been okay, but my far too crazy self didn't see quite clearly after that. I ripped his head off and threw it into the center of the room. She screamed a gurgling cry and lunged for me. I caught her with little effort. Her blood patched against my own bare chest as she tried to struggle against me. She was nothing more than a wild animal. Her eyes enveloped into their oblivion, black as she thrashed against me. Crazy. She was a brilliant crazy scientist.

Her reaction to my interference of her workspace was all I needed to see so I could summarize the lies that she had laid out up until this point. My Darling Sasha had lied and cheated to cover her tracks. She took opportunity in the events that unfolded before her and was gambling with her life in the sake of her work. She undoubtedly lied to the throne. She had even lied to me. What a clever vixen she was.

"Your father didn't really leave the walls, did he?" I asked with a theory in mind. If he had convicted his own wife for her experiments, I imagined his resolve would be no different towards his daughter. His crazy blood thirsty daughter who would never run but fight instead. There was no space for concern of family and loyalty in a person who was not entirely sane.

The mention of her father gave her a moment of pause. Her head jerked to the side as she looked somewhat ashamed. "He found out about this experimenting, didn't he?" I said pushing back her wild hair that was tarnished in vampire blood. She didn't flinch away from my touch. Her body eased slightly as the flow of adrenalin passed through. Her black eyes were gobbled up by her brown pupils. The mention of her father was a reality that could pull her back from her monstrous state.

"I was searching for an answer," she begun desperately explaining herself. "My mother's work had purpose," she pledged. Her line of thought was scattered. "I was her failure, but I can make better ones. Faster and stronger ones!" She sounded resolved and that fiery determination flashed through her eyes as she looked at me again. I wiped a smear of blood away from her cheek, totally intoxicated by the mass of crazy that had thrown herself onto me.

"Better what, Sasha Darling?" I had never been so curious by someone else's thought process other than my own. I wanted to hear her answer. I wanted to see where her curious and lethal mind led to. What was my Sasha craving more than anything else in this world? What was her mad hatter ambition? She paused momentarily as she held her breath. I doubted that she had ever expressed her deepest darkest secrets to anyone. Only perhaps the very people she experimented on. I wanted her to let me in. To submit to me and let me into her most volatile scheme. Her body tightened before she unhinged and admitted her crazy resolve.

"Hunters," she whispered. "Human weapons to kill the vampires and take us into the new world." Her eyes were crazed and my cock throbbed at the over ambitious statement. I pulled her hair back and looked down at those wild eyes that were pinned on me. She pressed a gun to my chest. My cock hardened in response and a low whimper came out of her as she felt it. I pressed it against her, as if demanding more answers. She whimpered as she pressed the gun harder into my chest. I didn't have to voice my question, there was an understanding between us that needed no words. "My father discovered what I was doing, and I had no choice…" She pressed down on me, her hips rolling in response.

"You killed him," I finished her sentence. I didn't care who she killed and why. It turned me on when my pet was willing to get her hands bloody for what she most desired. Even if it were her own family. Everyone could be discarded. It was the guarantee in this unfortunate life. It excited me that we had both killed our fathers for reasons that suited our own agenda. Yet another reason why my little mouse was as brilliantly wicked as me.

"Sasha Darling," I growled and let her see my fangs for what they were. The very abomination she hated. I was the one thing she despised most. I pressed my cock harder against her leather pants to feel the outline of her sweet lips. She pressed the gun harder against my chest as I pressed further against her. "I think you're batshit crazy but that enthralls me like you wouldn't believe." I spun her and slammed her back against the wall. The smells and horrors of the room simmered away in the distance. I was totally and inevitably enveloped in her scent and the wild craze to be deep inside of her.

"You'll kill me for this," she whispered.

"Oh, I won't. My brother would," I said leaning my head

into the scent of her neck and against her jagged scar. I licked it, the taste of her salty flesh making me shudder in delight. She melted into the motion as she sunk further on top of me. The only thing that came between us was those unbearably thin pants. Oh, and the gun. "Your secret can be my secret," I whispered. I grazed my sharp fangs up her neck. She submitted slightly by arching into the motion. I pinned her other hand beside her. The other side of her neck was a mixture of dry blood and the oozing trickle from where it reopened. The night of lush killings and adrenalin had us both wildly entangled in a desire that came after such appeasing fun. Her eyes were stark black on me as I brushed my nose against hers.

"Let me drive you crazy, Sasha Darling" I said, nipping at her lip where a small droplet of blood appeared. I looked at it with earnest greed. I knew her secret. She had a choice to either submit or kill me now. By the smell of her arousal and lack of any logic streaming through her now, I knew that the steely Sasha that first presented herself to me was now a buttery mess. And very woman. She was crazy. She had to submit to me now. I wanted it. I wanted to taste her and to be no longer denied my right. My right, to be inside of her as I treated her like a delicacy "Let me lavish in your sweetness," I purred, pressing myself against her again. Her hips rolled against me.

"I could kill you," she said in a soft whimper. But her body was telling me all I needed to know. Her heart raced rapidly. I could feel the heat from her pussy radiate over my cock that pressed against her. I could smell her.

"Well either fuck me or kill me Little Mouse, but don't make me wait." She pressed down on me, inciting a deep moan from me as I felt her on a better angle. She pointed the gun down and shot me in the foot. I didn't have time to make a consequential noise because her lips were already on mine, crushing into me like a wicked fire. Her blood was on the tip of her tongue pushing into me, forcing the taste of her down my throat.

She dropped the gun with speed and force trying to undo my loose pants. She'd pushed them down and my cock sprung free. She panted as she took a moment to look at its size. Her eyes glowered with hunger as she took my lips once again. I grabbed the side of her pants, ripping them off in one clean movement. I threw them onto the vampire that remained, using him as a coat hanger as I fisted Sasha's hair back.

The tip of my cock lapped in her sweet wetness. The smell of her wafted over me like a cannon of sweet perfume. I tore off the thin leather that would keep the rest of her body hidden from me. Beautiful. Her breasts were perfect and fit my palm. Scars scattered over her chest and between her breasts. They were the reminders of experiments her mother executed on her. She didn't flinch nor shy. I was entirely aroused and awed by her glory.

I cupped one of her breasts, pinching the nipple. She moaned and threw her head back slightly arching into my rhythm. The silver bullet that she had shot into my foot began to push out and heal. It was a clear message. *I want to fuck you, but I would kill you if I had the strength.* I thrusted into her hard, fast, and unexpecting. She cried in pain, wrapping her legs around me to hold on. I shuddered, reminding myself not to come inside of her in that one splitting moment. Never had I felt so at ease or sane. Never had I felt so content and with purpose in the world. This crazy wild scientist would be the end of me. I cocked a smile as she moaned and rolled her eyes back into her head, focusing on me.

I took a shallow breath. Not that I needed to breath but that I was finally relieved. The tension that has been building in this game we had been playing would finally come undone. None of this made any fucking sense. And yet we were both mad in our own way where inevitably it did.

Love wasn't a notion either of us were capable of. But there was madness and we understood ownership. We were monopolizing one another. Whether she liked it or not, I would never let her leave my sight alive. She looked at me as if reading my mind and kissed me again, this time biting down on my lip with her very human teeth. The taste of my blood mixed with hers, pulsed another hardening urge through my cock. I looked down uncertain if it were possible for it to grow any more for this greedy vixen. Blood of our enemies and her still healing wounds was now smearing on her stomach. The entire room now smelled purely of Sasha.

I stared at her inviting neck that pulsed, enticing me, begging to be taken. "Please," I begged for the first lover that I had ever asked permission from. I began to fuck her out of her mind. I pumped for the second time and then a third. I bounced her on my dick hard and fast against the wall. Small fragments of rubble broke free from the cemented wall during every thrust. I pumped into her once again. And again. And again. Until she gave me permission.

"Yes," was her husky response as I tried to contain my savageness. With her permission, I bit into her neck, my fangs piercing and delighting in her pulse. Her blood swelled into my mouth as I curled inside of her once again. She moaned in exhilarated bliss. My Darling Sasha was dripping in my mouth, my tongue rolling around the punctures that I had formed. Her taste was off, not like any other human that I had. She tasted of metal—of a creature that had been fiddled with and reprogramed. I took another bite into her, lavishing in the taste. Because this was my Sasha in all her glory.

Crazier than I could have ever begged for in another. I pumped, envisioning that we were on that battle ground again–killing as we had together. I continued to fuck her as if we had never stopped in that place. I was envisioning fucking her against the burning building of the enemies we had just slaughtered together. She moaned as her lips pursed around me and a sweet wet wave swept through her.

I continued to pump harder, conscious that I could break her but just when I thought I was about to, her nails raked down my back and she begged for more. I gave her what she wanted and continued to relish in her taste.

The humans behind us continued to shudder in fear. Their sobs only added to this wicked affair. Nothing else mattered now that I had her. Nothing ever would. I collected her in my arms and splayed her on the gurney, continuing to pump into her. She held onto the side of the bars, the wheels creaking back and forth as I fucked her. I leaned over her to lick at the wound I had inflicted on her. I kissed down her jagged scar gently adoring her imperfection.

I bit into her left breast enjoying the softer and plumper skin that was entirely woman. Another wave came crashing over my cock as she moaned out a cry. Her breathing began to change as she panted and begged for more. She was exhausted. The blood loss and battle had entirely depleted her. I grabbed her and held her close to my chest. With speed that would always outrun her, I jumped through the hole I had crafted in the ceiling and placed her into the single bed in her bedroom.

"What are you doing?" She asked in a haze of disappointment. I wavered a cocky grin. Oh, how I could make her beg for more but I was too impatient. I wouldn't stop lavishing in her now, no matter how exhausted she was. I held down her arms as I pressed my face between her thighs.

"It's been a long day, Sasha Darling. You need to rest," I inhaled the smell of her essence that was now a mixture of us combined. "So let me do what I can to help put you at ease." And then I kissed her lips gently and began to lick at the very core of her heat. Of which she would have sweet dreams tonight.

CHAPTER
II

TWO MAD HATTERS IN A POD

I SAT ON THE FLOOR against the ceiling-tall mirror watching Sasha as she slept. I was still smiling. I had pleased her to the point of exhaustion. She was sprawled on her bed naked and vulnerable for only my eyes to see. Her wounds had begun to stitch and heal together.

The artificial sun programmed inside of the dome began to rise and shine through the broken edges of the window. She mumbled and stirred as she woke. I continued to watch her as she buried herself further beneath the blanket. Her eyes shot open. She jumped upright, alarmed by my presence in her room. She was backed against her bedframe. When she saw me, her body sagged in ease and exhaustion. Her pounding heart began to ease as her steely self regained composure. It must've been a long time since my little mouse woke up to that of company.

"I thought you would've left by now," she said looking

around the room that was half destroyed. The sheets and feathers from her pillow had been torn apart, from both of our doing. Scratch marks raked down the wall, mostly from her. The bedframe had busted apart and creaked as she shuffled. She looked around as if trying to recall the night before.

"I have no reason to leave. What I want right now is in this room. I don't plan on going anywhere," I said huskily. It was both a threat and intensity of endearment.

She rubbed the back of her head and looked at me with those steely brown eyes that never offered emotion. "You're the very thing I despise the most."

"And you are nothing more than food to me and yet here I am... fucking my loaf of bread," I said in reply. She continued to stare, and I smiled hoping it would infect her. "Come on, that was funny. Who cares what we are, Sasha Darling. You have a wicked mind and so do I. We both have a body-"

"And yours is dead. A dead body," she interrupted me.

"And yours is a mutated and modified shell. You're not exactly organic yourself, Darling," I chided back not at all prickly by her seething words. They aroused me even further. Watching the hatred and passion roll off her in waves was aesthetic to me. "And besides, my dead body certainly seemed to fill a void that you've never known to exist before."

She looked away and gritted her teeth. She sat on her knees with her hands clasped before her. "Why me? Why did you of all people, a crazy vampire prince, take interest in me?"

"Because I do what I want and follow what takes my fancy," I said effectively. "I don't know how to express in normal human lingo or express myself with profound words. But I know when I want something to be mine. And I take it. That darkness that is in you, arouses me beyond belief. I've had many vampire lovers, none of which has held my interest. Most of them, no more than a day. Together I can envision us burning down cities and fucking on their tallest buildings. I've never considered having a partner in crime such as that. Dare I say, for your woman ears, that you might be special to me."

She scoffed. "I experiment on vampires to find a way to kill your kind. Aren't you concerned I will turn on you?"

I shrugged my shoulders. "Your madness isn't limited to just vampires. You have humans down there as well against their will. You just don't play well with others and are justifying your acts as a bold statement for the greater good." The sun began to slowly creep in, cascading in a line to come between us.

She gritted out in frustration. "I only experiment on humans to find better ways to make Hunters. People will thank me in the future. My kind, will thank me when I find the answers."

I exhaled for dramatic response. Oh, how sickly maddening she was. How I had heard such crazed speeches before and the outcome had always been the same. "People like you never find the answers that you're after. Your mind is simply so twisted that you don't know how to be anything other than a monster. One day your experimenting went too far beyond redemption. So why stop at the vampires... why stop at the humans? Your colorful mind will never stop crafting abomination after abomination because you will always find a way to justify it. You think because it is 'science' that it is just." She went to interrupt me but I continued, speaking over her. "But my lovely monster, I adore that and encourage it. We might be mad in our own way and be the monster I may, I am the only one in this world that will be aroused by your destructive nature. We're both monsters. Just admit it."

She looked at me for a moment longer. She stood up and walked over to me with those predatory eyes that missed nothing. Her body flexed as she walked over. She was so perfectly muscled and dangerous. Sasha was a woman of decision and action. My little mouse was an opportunist and quickly calculated the most beneficial outcome to her cause. She was as calculated as my brother but as ruthless as my own nature. She leaned towards me and inhaled my scent. A very primal and animalistic response, even for her. "How long have you been hiding that wild beast inside of you?" I asked, curious at what age her parents might've seen the consequence of her mother's experiments.

"For a very long time," she said huskily. She leaned in and bit the bottom of my lip, pulling at it. I went to pull her on top of me, but she hissed at me. This was her time and her action to initiate. This was her own dance and pace as she came to agree to the terms of our twisted games that we would enjoy. My cock was already throbbing hard as her breasts dangled before me, luscious and ready for the taking. But I would play her game. I would let her think that she was in control and that she could obtain me of all vampires, as a submissive. This was on her terms.

Puppet. Puppeteer. She and I were the same. We always had to be in control. But if I wanted my hard cock to release inside of her now, I had to play along with this little dance for the time being. Let the feral animal come to me until she would obediently be petted. It was only a matter of time; and time that I was willing to create for her.

"When my father saw what my mother had done," she said half crazed. "He hated her. Couldn't understand what she had done to me and the children. But she only wanted to make us stronger."

She grabbed my wrists and pinned them above me with force. I liked where this was going. "And did she make you stronger?" I asked rhetorically.

"Yes," she said as she nibbled at my ear and licked up the side of my face in maddening ownership. The warmth of her chest smothered me with her scent while I looked down at the jagged scar that would beautifully mark her body forever more.

"Where did you get that scar?" I growled in response to her own primal creature. She looked at me from the side as if deciding to keep her secrets or to share them with me. Would she permit me into her world entirely?

"Another child. When we were in the same room, not all of them mixed well with the experiments and venom." Venom? "One attacked me and ripped into my throat. So, I killed her. This scar is what remains. She was the first human I'd ever killed, and I wasn't even sad. In fact, it bewildered me. How was I stronger than her? What was the difference in our might? How could I become stronger, and if not, craft the strongest human ever made?" I understood where her craziness had begun and how it shaped my little mouse into the predator that she was. She nibbled at my lip again, rubbing her breasts against me.

"Did you say venom, Sasha Darling?" I muffled. Was vampire venom the formula that started this maddening notion? Were they using the very essence that they spited? She edged to the side as she nipped at my neck hard enough to draw blood. For someone who hated the very existence of vampires, her very predatory nature was exactly like a newborn.

"From vampires," she admitted. "That's how my mother started crafting our kind. She injected us with the genetics and venom from vampires." I arched an eyebrow in admiration of her mother's ideal. We used our venom to immobilize and turn humans if we so desired. I'd never considered the possibility of one human mind trying to transform that into an entirely different species. I had to give credit where it was due. Where the humans lacked in strength, they inevitably made up for it in innovation.

Sasha's eyes had gone entirely black. The talk of her mother's experiments and the beginning of her creation might've traumatized most but for Sasha; it was an awakening to her darker self and the entirety of who she was now. She was excited by the possibilities and aroused by having the very thing she so greatly despised be hard for her and strapped to the wall just for her to fuck.

She straddled me, groaning as her wet lips parted over my cock and moistened around me. She grabbed my wrists and led them to trace over the side of her chiseled stomach as she bounced on my cock. She led my hands down her waist and rested them on her hips. She moaned into my mouth as she dragged her tongue against my fangs and licked at her lips totally aroused. The smell of her left me parting my mouth for more as she leaned away from me, teasing me.

"For the few of us who survived her experiments, we plan on running into the new world that parallels our own." Her words came in hot and heavy pants as she continued to bounce on me.

"Do you?" I pulled back her hair reminding her that she would never break free of my grasp. "And how long have you been planning this daring escape?" I asked having enough of her joy ride on my cock. I lifted her, despite her forceful push back and pinned her against the wall. I thrusted into her, now having total control. As it should've been from the start.

"Ever since the moment I walked in to have an audience with you." She said and whimpered into my mouth as I thrust into her hard. An opportunist, that's what my clever little mouse was. She weighed the pros and cons of everything that had been transpiring over the past few weeks. I drove into her hard, harder than ever to remind her who was fucking whom. She would never have the luxury to escape these walls unless I permitted it. Just as we have been doing these past few weeks. It would only ever happen because I would allow it. I slammed into her again. She groaned as the wall behind her began to break apart, chipping, in time with my thrusts.

She was mine and wasn't going anywhere. I would fuck her into oblivion every day so she could never use her legs to escape my clutches.

"You're mine," I growled in case she didn't hear my message loud and clear through my actions.

I put my fingers in her mouth and she bit down—hard. She licked over the tips of my fingers with her tongue. Her hips rolled over me as she moaned. I parted her ass cheeks with my other hand and dared to provoke her asshole with a finger. She sunk into it, groaning as her second hole expanded over me.

"For however long this might last... maybe," she whispered in pure ecstasy. She bit down on my fingers once again. I licked over the edges of her jagged scar, nipping at my meal.

"My Darling, I will make it last forever," I said and bit into the jagged remains of the horrors that was once done to her as a child. Her entire body clenched around me in pain, until she released and relaxed into me. I thrusted into her again and began to feed on her. I would never let her go.

CHAPTER 12

TICK TOCK THE BIRD IS DEAD

IT WAS AN OMINOUS FEELING having Sasha sprawled out over me naked. I had fucked her into exhaustion yet again. Blood smeared from floor to ceiling as we lay in her single bed. I stared up at the ceiling, foreign to such contact. We just finished fucking and yet I still wanted her skin against mine. I wondered if I could stitch our skins together so that she could never escape. I held onto her tightly, then released slightly before my nails would draw blood. She was such a tiny fragile human. I could kill her in an instant but wanted to see her thrive in her darkness instead. I wanted her to prosper but only under my watch. Her heartbeat drummed over my non-existing one. It unsettled me by how much her rhythmic beat put my body in a state of rest. She was a threat to me and an overbearing new weakness that I couldn't yet muster the glee to kill.

Her eyes didn't flutter open, but I could sense that she

was awake. Her dead weight lightened, and her breathing changed. She rested for a moment more before speaking. "You know that Oppollo wasn't going to move his hand or retaliate until you did what you did."

"What *we* did," I corrected. "I know." I smiled. It would be my brother's problem now. I was excited to see the outcome.

"Oppollo is focused on reaching the other world. Our world and existence are only a pen to keep the vampires in. Why do you think he hadn't acted sooner?"

I looked at her from the corner of my eye. Her nail scratched down between my pecks, she drew blood each time and it quickly healed. She dragged her nail down again in a soothing manner.

"It seems my crazy scientist knows a lot more about what's beyond the walls than guarding them. Where did you find all this out?" I was impressed by her ability to decipher such information despite being so limited in freedom. They weren't even allowed outside the walls and yet, somehow, she had crafted over the years a way to source such information. It made sense; my brother might've even mentioned it to me. Not that I listened, nor did I care.

She sprung up resting her head on her propped elbow. "Do you really want to know?" she said giddily. She brightened like a child, excited that she could share her masterful creation. I pushed back part of the golden waves of her hair that cascaded in front of her eyes.

"I want to know everything that is crafted from that beautiful mind, Sasha," I said. I wanted to know every wicked detail and process of how she worked.

"So I-" Alarms swelled throughout the city. Sasha stopped talking and looked outside the window. I didn't look away from her. We wouldn't be able to see anything from the bay of her window. No, the commotion would be beyond the wall. I smiled wickedly, because I knew outside the walls would be a galloping heap of vampires coming to attack the very Kingdom my brother so proudly reigned over. And it was all under attack because of my actions. Glorious fun.

"I guess Oppollo is on his way," I charmed a smile at her. Bloodbath. Fucking a mad scientist. War. My perfect, ideal week.

A mixture of emotion rolled over her usually stern face. I furrowed my eyebrows in confusion. "Translate whatever you are calculating in your head to me, Sasha Darling." I wanted to understand her every thought and action. She furrowed her eyebrows and pushed away from me. Her thoughts were somewhere else entirely.

"I need to gather my research papers," she said and jumped out of bed. I grabbed her wrist before she could leave. I wasn't letting her go until she gave me an explanation. She hissed and noticed me for the first time since the alarms began to sound. "Oppollo is ruthless. He will burn this city to the ground if your brother can't defend this city. I knew that when I came with you to antagonize him. I have to gather my papers. I'll flee this city with my team and findings. No matter what, my research must survive for the new world that we'll soon enter."

I raised my eyebrows. My crazy scientist spoke significantly of the new world that paralleled ours. It made me curious if she knew more than what she led on or if she was simply an idealist. Foremost, I asked. "You plan on fleeing the battle?" I was infuriated that she didn't plan on taking part of the fun with me. This could be our glorious bloodshed together.

"I plan on continuing my research and escaping into the

human world. *The real one.* My mother did it and so can I." The alarms continued to run through the city, heightening in noise. I could sense my brother's guards gather outside Sasha's apartment. When they stepped closer, they were startled by her security system that would keep them back. I knew that my brother had sent them to take me. He would always have me on the frontline of his battles. As I always desired.

"Oppollo's men won't break through the wall," I said confidently. Not if I was standing in their way.

"I don't think Oppollo's only target is this kingdom." *So, I would stop him and whatever other goal he had in mind.* "You're not unkillable," she said pulling out of my grasp so she could put her leather attire on.

"Careful Darling, that almost sounds like concern," I said as I found my loose trousers on the floor. Fancy that, I was preparing for an epic battle in my PJs. She zipped up her sleeveless shirt and looked over her shoulder. She tied her hair into a tight ponytail. Before we went our separate ways, I threatened her, "If you attempt to run away from me, I'll find you."

"To do what, Kyran?" She asked huffing and raking her leather pants on her creamy white legs. "To kill me or join me in a world that you probably won't be able to survive?"

"Which ever one comes sooner. But the latter sounds far more exciting." She stared at me in contemplation. Someone shouted out my name from outside. It distracted neither of us.

"Is that what you plan on doing? A vampire prince following a human into a world with real sunlight and the uncertainty of survival. Are you suicidal?" She asked now grabbing for her weapons. I came to her side with lightning speed and grabbed her wrist. I jarred her chin to look up at me with unrelenting force.

"I do whatever I want. But remember, you're *mine*. There is no way I'll let you escape with a gang of your little hunter pals where you can gang bang without me. I'll find you," I threatened. "And understand that if you try to ever escape me, I'll destroy everything around you and all that you've lived and worked for."

"Somehow," she hissed. "Your threats have little meaning when your cock is still rock hard against me." I looked down at my bulge that was indeed poking into her. I took her lips into mine and pressed my tongue against hers in dominance. She fought back as always.

"Threat. Promise. Call it whatever you like. But you won't escape me little mouse. Now do your job on the wall well," I mused and bit at her lip to draw blood. I walked away towards the broken window.

"Don't have your unbeating heart ripped out," she hissed from behind me. I charmed a smile at my devilish woman and jumped through the window to reach those who dared ruin my sex rendezvous.

One of the vampires began to offer me a report. I ushered him away. "Yeah, yeah. Oppollo's on his way. Blah blah blah," I said. They split away for me, making room so I could walk down the center of their formation. "Has the King yet appeared?" My brother would either hide in his castle, preaching bullshit that he believed in my ability to take the frontline; or he would lead by example like the warrior that he, only sometimes chose to be, to showcase his boring leadership.

"He's positioned at the entrance of the wall, Prince Kyran," the vampire reported. Ew. The formality irked me every time. He shuffled uncomfortably away when his gaze dropped to my massive hard on. I had no shame.

I made my way to the front wall where the gates were already opened and ready for our troops to disperse. The human wall guards prepared formation with barrels of flames, arrows, and machinery they'd never had to use before. Amell's vampire army rustled silently, waiting for the signal to leave the front gates. The natural moonlight shone through the large wooden doors. Such a rarity to see them open and welcoming in the natural cold breeze of the outside.

I scaled the wall and jumped onto the highest peak where my brother stood watching with his keen sight within a small guarded tower. I had to admit it was all theatrically beautiful. My attack had been unannounced, fast, and relentless. Now this was slow, flamboyant, and on a larger scale. They were practically announcing themselves.

"Are you happy now?" Amell said with his head held high. He looked past his nose down at the piles of vampires that came our way in the distance.

"Very," I said satisfied. He gritted his teeth. He still wouldn't dare look at me. I could feel his hatred for me waving off him. *Boohoo I started a war for my brother.*

"Perhaps once this is over and done with brother, we should consider going our separate ways for a while," he said and then finally looked at me. I could see the hatred in his eyes. The look was no different to the usual every time we had decided to part ways for a few years. Which meant I was to make myself disappear.

"Should I leave before the fight begins?" I asked pointing to the back gate.

"You wouldn't want to leave even if I ordered it," he scoffed. Order this, order that, his words were as boring as ever. *All hail boring King Amell.* I agreed, I had been within the wall for far too long. Finally, what I had been waiting for had come. I stayed here for the battle and now it was on our doorstep.

"Where is Galador?" I asked. Suspicious that his usual ass kisser wasn't about. I kept a keen sense on Sasha's whereabouts at all times. She was positioned at the wall already. I looked down the stream of blank faces as they watched on as the army approached us. It was rather dramatic considering only two of us took out so many of them and they responded with an entire army. Weapons were strapped to her body and a small bag dangled on her hip. I imagined that was what contained all her life's work. So, my little mouse was serious on scurrying away.

Down the many rows of humans, Sasha was yelling at the other human guards, instructing them into position. I charmed a wicked smile as she delegated orders and planned on fleeing herself. I puffed my chest higher. Yep, that was the woman I was fucking.

"I positioned him on the other side of the wall to guard the rear in case they circle around," Amell said. An interesting place to put a vampire who acted as an advisor instead of a warrior. I side glanced my brother, suspicious.

"Perhaps you would like to lead your men?" I offered him, gesturing for him to take the first step onto the battlefield. Recklessness wasn't his forte, it had always been self-preservation and winning calculations.

"Or perhaps you should do what you do best, Brother, it's never stopped you before," he countered with a harsh grimace. I charmed a smile. Hickory, Dickory, Dock. I jumped over the ledge of the tower not waiting for further invitation. As soon as my feet hit the ground my brother raised his arm in signal. The barrage of vampire warriors followed my lead and flooded through the front gates.

Now this would be fun. I kept an acute awareness on Sasha's position as I left Grand Klaus's walls. I would not let her run away nor would I let anyone dare strike my toy down. The ground was damp and sloshed as we trampled over plants that still attempted to survive in the cold terrain. Animals darted into different directions and away from the land that would soon be a gravesite. We ran towards the masses of soldiers and collided with a crackle of breaking bones. Fangs, weapons, and nails collided. There was a barrage and wall of vampires that smashed into one another. I sliced through the masses with purposeful strikes. Every single strike was deadly.

I avoided their silver bullets and cruel intentions. Some of those who followed me from behind weren't as fortunate. I looked amongst the masses in search of Oppollo. His men continued to obstruct my path and remain as a distraction. I ripped the ribcage of one from his body and busted it over the head of another, glorifying in the act. I howled in the moonlight of the blood that was splattering over my bare chest. Not blood of mine but that of my enemies.

An arrow shot for me. I side stepped it, catching it as it flew past. I twisted and spun, throwing it back into the archer's chest and marking home. He immediately sagged into a rotting corpse. His remains were torn apart by those who trampled over him and continued to fight.

I continued shredding through them, aware of Sasha's fast movement and change of positioning. She was heading for the rear of the wall. I'd never been so in tune or aware of another's presence, especially over a such a long distance. My instinct irked me back towards the city. Something was off. This wasn't just a blood sport and battle. I couldn't see Oppollo anywhere and Sasha was changing course drastically like she always did in a hunt.

I growled in frustration having to pull away from my amusement. There was confusion amongst some of the soldiers as I changed course. They continued their own battle and slashing through the masses. I left them behind without a second thought. I ran around the edges of the wall tracing Sasha's steps.

Arrows and flames propelled from the wall and through the skies above me, lighting the natural night. I rounded the back of the wall and continued past that. I could sense that Sasha had fled the walls. On the rear station, a gaping hole and numerous panels had been opened in the back of the wall. The Dome had come down but none of Oppollo's men were near to take advantage. There was no evident damage on the exterior which meant the panels would've been taken down from the inside. Human guards tried to close the panels one by one to recover its defenses. Only an exceptional fast team would be able to open all those panels at once; which meant it was either vampires from the inside or Sasha's little Hunter family.

I could sense that Sasha was still on the hunt, further past the forestry and mountains behind Grand Klaus. I traced her scent and footsteps. She was amongst others. It was a mixture of humans, vampires, and the similar scent of Sasha's metallic one—other hunters. Her movements halted. The rest surrounding her and then the smell of blood began to flood the air. I rounded a clump of hibernating trees in the cold weather and looked back and forth in disarray. I could smell that she was close, but I couldn't see them. I circled the rock formation in front of me but still couldn't see them. There was no entrance to the cave that I was certain she was within.

Clashing noises came from within the cave and the smell of blood continued to stain the air. Then it hit me—Sasha's blood. I readied my shoulder and ran at the stone. I barged through it but instead of it splintering apart or self-splattering against it; I went straight through with no resistance. I ran into a vampire that splattered against the wall. *That wasn't purposeful but fabulous either way.*

A mixture of Galador's and my brother's men fought against one another. A few human hunters were fighting off Oppollo's men but evidently outnumbered. Against the back wall was a large waterfall. It gushed as men ran into it. They returned after only a few seconds indicating that it was clear on the other side. I paused for a moment, realizing that Oppollo was in this very room and before my eyes, his silhouette vanished into the waterfall after receiving the all clear. His presence, his smell, his might, his everything, entirely disappeared from this world.

It dawned on me. This was it. The place that took our kind into the next, the parallel world we knew of but could never reach. Oppollo had used this battle as a decoy to step into the new world. He didn't care about the outcome of his entire army, he hinged it all on this one opportunity. How had my brother been so oblivious that the entrance to the new world was so close to us this whole time.

Sasha's gasp broke my focus. She was pinned against the wall as Galador dove his fangs into her neck. I grabbed his face from behind and ripped open his jaw, flinging him back in rage.

I couldn't make sense of any of it. All four parties fought one another. There were no alliances amongst the warriors from Grand Klaus. My brother's men continued to fight one another. The remains of Sasha's mutated people were fighting to stay alive amongst the room of vampires that they could never outmatch. Galador's jaw hung by its hinges. He growled in response, slashing at one of the hunters who ran past him. His nails dragged down the hunter's face and down his chest.

"You've always had the tendency to get in my way. And

now your bitch of a girlfriend is causing more issue," he said limply as his jaw reattached itself.

Sasha collected herself, trying to lean against the wall behind me. Blood oozed out of her neck and trailed down her shoulder. I kept her in the corner of my eye. If she was going to attack me, she would've done it already. Her legs buckled beneath her and I knew that the bite from Galador had taken its toll. He wasn't like the young vampires we had fought before. And she had fought an army of vampires only the day before. It had taken its toll on her human body.

"Are you working for Oppollo?" I asked to clarify the situation. Either way I was going to kill him. His jaw stitched back into place and he pointed behind me.

"And betray your brother?! That *thing*," he said pointing to Sasha. "Was the one that led Oppollo to this cave!"

"Okay," I said and smiled. I'd always hated Galador anyway. I ran for him. He snarled in response and prepared himself. One of the hunters shot a bullet at him, and like the same mistake that I had made, Galador moved only slightly to avoid it. The bullet exploded into silver splinters and threw him against the wall. As soon as he staggered to move, two of my brother's men jumped on him and began to tear him a part. So Galador was loyal to my throne. Some of my brother's men were working for Oppollo and as for the Hunters...

One of the hunters raised a gun at me. "Stop!" Sasha exclaimed. But it was too late. I wouldn't allow anyone who raised a weapon against me to survive. Even if they were her beloved and own kind. In fact, I wouldn't let any of them survive. There were consequences to Sasha's daring abandonment. I dodged the bullet and ran sideways along the inside of the cave. I slashed through them bearing my fangs and ripping into each of their necks. I tore apart the final human as I dove into his neck. They weren't nearly as strong as my Darling Sasha. *They* were her mother's failures. His scream was a beautiful wave of music to my ears.

Sasha threw a dagger at me. "Stop!" She screamed. But I wouldn't listen. She had betrayed me. There was consequence to that. And I wouldn't stop at that. I wouldn't allow any of those who betrayed my brother to follow Oppollo into the new world to survive either. No one was to whisper of the secrets to this cave. Few had already slipped through into the waterfall behind Oppollo. Some had even run back out, frightful of what they'd seen. As they tried to run back through the entrance of the cave, I slaughtered them.

I grabbed the heart of the remaining vampire and threw it away and into the waterfall. Let this new world have the decaying heart of the vampires which lived on the other side.

"Stop!" Sasha said as I approached the final human who was dragging herself towards the waterfall. The insides of her stomach were daring to fall out from where a vampire had slashed her open. I stepped towards her and looked Sasha dead in the eye as I pressed my foot against the woman's head and stomped it into the ground.

Sasha's eyes were her usual intense steely brown. No tears or emotion. "Who will you experiment on now?" I antagonized. She hissed at me, as she tried to stand on her own. "I told you that I wouldn't let you go. And yet you orchestrated quite the operation here." I waved my finger around, impressed. "Invisible rock thing?"

She huffed and raised her top lip in anger. She stood tall with her hands by her sides. "My mother created it." I shook my head in approval. Her mother's advancements in technology was something this world could never handle. *Good job mother-in-law.*

As Sasha kept a steady eye on me, I wondered if she would attack me first. She was the only survivor from this expedition and her fate was in my hands. I couldn't smell fear on her. This woman didn't care about such things nor did my presence rattle her as it should. I pinned her against the wall by the throat.

"So, you've been in cahoots with Oppollo. I wasn't anticipating that," I said gallantly. I loosened my grip on her throat so she could speak. Part of her hair cascaded around my knuckles from where her hair had been cleanly sliced in the fight.

"I told you he planned on escaping into the other world," she said condescending.

"Yea but you lacked in detail my little mouse," I said squeezing her throat once again. "So, you've unleashed a ruthless vampire into the world of unsuspecting humans. Isn't that against what you so very much believe in?"

"My mother-" I crushed down on her throat so she couldn't finish the sentence.

"You did all this because Mommy told you to?" I irked.

"I told you that I would leave," she said, now scratching at my throat. "What do you want from me, Kyran?"

I released her and she barely caught herself from dropping to the floor. Did she even have to ask the question? I snorted at her ignorance. The cave began to stink of the dead.

"Well I've made it very clear!" I snapped at her, irritated that I would have to summarize something so simple to such a clever woman. "You're mine. It seems that my little pet thought she could stray farther than what I permitted her and that makes me angry. I knew that you were looking for a way into this new Utopia of yours, but I thought it was an unrealistic ambition. To then secretly have this entire project planned and to be in cahoots with the enemy while defending my brother's Kingdom…" I paused, processing it while I said it out loud. She watched me steadily and looked at the waterfall from the corner of her eye. I wondered if she would be so bold as to make a run for it. That aroused me. She would be the only daring mouse to continually try and run away from me.

"I'm rather impressed," I decided, casually putting my hands into the pockets of my loose pants. I began to laugh wickedly, finding the humor in all of this. This was actually perfect. There was no greater insult to my brother than being undermined by the very pet I had only recently adopted. It was brilliant. This whole time she had been scheming such a brilliant plot and even I was oblivious to the performance and stage. How this woman existed just for my pleasure, baffled me. "Oh, how I adore your clever mind, Darling Sasha," I scooped her face into my hands. I was fixated on this fragile human who at no point had begged for her life. She stood by her decision despite my consequential reaction.

"This is utter madness. I've hardly explained anything to you and yet you praise me," she shook her head. Her body still wobbled from the blood loss. She looked over my shoulder at the decaying vampire bodies and the humans that still bled out. She pressed her hand against mine and closed her eyes.

"They don't matter," I said. "None of them matter. Only you and I." I didn't care for how many creatures came between us. I would kill anyone who tried to step between me and what was mine. If she considered the only thing that could truly separate us was this world and the next… then I was willing to prove her wrong and keep her chained to my side. I looked at the waterfall and back at her. "If you want this so badly. Then let's go together."

She shook her head and offered me her usual matter of fact expression. "You might not survive the new world. I don't know what's beyond that wall."

"And yet you let Oppollo and his army stride straight through," I said pointing after them. I wrapped my hand around her waist and jolted her into a dance. She hissed at the pain. I didn't entirely stop my gleeful dance but slowed the pace. My fragile Sasha daring to complain about a private dance with me, the Prince of Grand Klaus. "Tell me in words why. Speak."

Her eyes whirled around as she breathed heavily censoring out the pain. "If you came with me, I don't know what my mother might try to do to you."

"That's not the answer I'm after, Sasha Darling. Besides, I think it's time you break free from your dearest mother's shadow. Now tell me what I want to hear," I said circling her again and pinning her against the wall. "Tell me," I growled. Her body heat pressed against the coldness of my own. My body thrummed with exhilaration at the prospect of how she would word it. I pressed my lips against hers. My tongue pressed against hers as she tried to fight for dominancy. She fisted the tops of my loose pants as she moaned into my mouth. Her breath was hot and bloody. Her body was always a quickfire response.

I pulled away offering her space for breath. Her eyes were entirely consumed in oblivion. She responded to my monster as I had hers. I wanted to hear her say it. "I don't want my mother touching what's mine," she growled from low in her belly. I replicated the growl as her words soaked into my every pore. *Hers.* I had finally won. I had obtained and captured my pet that was a crazy mad scientist. I had finally found someone who could rival me with her quipped tongue as much as her crazy brilliant mind.

"That's why I tried to leave without you," she admitted. I laughed. What a childish notion. It was more comical that she thought she'd get away with it.

"Oh, my little mouse, I told you that I'd never set you free again." I crushed my mouth against hers again. I rolled my hard cock against her, my body wanting to claim what was mine once again. Again, and again.

A small gadget was thrown through the wall. A low ticking noise began to beep behind me. I looked over my shoulder at the balled device that was flashing red.

"It's a bomb," she said and grabbed my hand. "One of the Hunters were instructed to throw it from the outside to destroy the connection between this world and the next."

She limply tugged me towards the waterfall. "I don't know if you'll survive this new world," she admitted.

"Oh, but my Darling, if I do, think of the wicked fun to be had," I smiled at all the prospects. "I can even help you with your research. I'll catch your test subjects so you can focus on your experiments at home," I said nudging her shoulder. She sheepishly smiled; her eyes still entirely swallowed by darkness. It was the first time I had ever seen her so brilliantly smile. We would walk into the unknown together and prepare to have a hell of a time. "Perhaps we should discuss turning you into a vampire soon, my Dear."

We walked through the water that rushed over and cleansed our blood splattered body. She added without fear as we began our journey into the new world, "I still despise your kind."

I clutched my nails in further so that she began to bleed. A gentle reminder that she was still mine and that I would never let her go. "But oh my Darling, how we like to fuck."

ABOUT THE AUTHOR

'Kia is a Token, no, she is THE Token of Vampire & Paranormal books.'

~ 5 STAR Reviewer.

Kia grew up in the Darling Downs Region in Queensland, Australia. Graduating High School, she pursued a career in freelance journalism. In 2014, having always had a passion for writing fiction, she decided to follow her dream of becoming an accomplished author.

Now living in Edinburgh, Scotland Kia has a can do attitude, a strong will and the touch of kindness that makes it hard not to fall in love with her. Announced 'The Best New Author of 2015' by AusRomToday, and being awarded numerous awards, she has no intentions of stopping. Kia Carrington-Russell is definitely the new author to be looking out for.

Learn more about Kia at www.kiacarrington-russell.com and follow @kia_crystal on Instagram.

OTHER BOOKS

FROM INTERNATIONAL BESTSELLING AUTHOR
KIA CARRINGTON-RUSSELL

Token Huntress

Esmore is one of the best; a Token in her Hunter Guild. After leading her team into the rubble remains of San Francisco and into an ambush, Esmore admitted her own sacrifice and defeat to protect her people.

Esmore went from being Token Huntress and leading her team to a life captured and hidden within the Vampire Council by a Vampire, Chase who claimed that she was his familiar.

In the year of 2,341, Esmore fights for her survival and the goal to maintain humanity from being entirely destroyed by the vampires who overpowered them those many years ago.

Dark. Romantic. Dangerous. Action Packed. Your tainted obsession starts today....

The Shadow Minds Journal:

In this world, there are creatures lurking in the shadows. As a child, I once played with them. As a teenager, I began to fear them and became victim to their attacks. As an adult, I now realize that no matter how much I try to escape the grasp of this world, I was inevitably born into it.

Now reborn as a Guardian in the year of 2986, Vivian Lair must uphold the treaty between Angels and Demons on the human world and city of Shabeah. Contracted to seven demons who she can shift into while taking direct orders from the Underworld Lord, Haymen, it wasn't exactly her ideal rebirth. Involving herself with the Angel of War, Gabe is even worse.

Still fighting those who try to possess her during her sleep, Vivian must now record and try to hunt the Volv through the Shadow Minds Journal. Now stuck between the hatred and lust of two of the most powerful entities in all worlds, Vivian is involved inevitably in the upcoming conflict.

Blood. Lust. War. She must kill before being killed.

My Escort Collection:

A collection of the Best Selling contemporary series that includes: My Escort, My Exception and My Expectation. Clover is personal assistant to Debra Coorman, the merciless boss of Candice fashion magazine. The bright lights of New York are dim for Clover, who is tormented by a work schedule like no other. Debra is relentless in her determination to demean Clover. For once, Clover dares to play Debra's games, and intends to prove her wrong at the next glittering event. With mixed emotions, Clover contacts a male escort, Damon. If his velvet voice over the phone is anything to go by, Clover knows her money will be well spent. But when Damon appears at her door, something unexpected happens. The taunts and the games begin. Who is truly going to win at this game?

Aroused: Taming Himself

"Remember my name because you will be begging me for more. This is my promise to you."

Meet Hayden Zilch: entrepreneur, sports manager, investor. Cocky, tantalizing, and an utter womanizer. He is a man who loves pleasuring women. He can show you a world you have only fantasied about.

So what happens when this sex-mad womanizer decides to finally find The One?

Starting off with a list of five women, Hayden sets out to learn the difference between lust and love. His adventures have him laughing, crying in pain, and begging on his knees as he battles to tame himself. Can Hayden really control himself around these five beautiful temptresses?

Taming Himself is the first in this five-book series which tells the story of Hayden's search for both love and pleasure.

Phantom Wolf

A book that is so dynamic and can pull my emotions free so easily is a 5 star novel.

★★★★★ - *Paranormal Trance Reviews*

Sia is a Phantom Wolf. Neither dead nor alive--and rotting from the inside--she is on the edge of her curse. Once a Phantom Wolf has been created, they hunt their blood pack and slaughter all their loved ones. Except for Sia, who woke years after her death to find herself rampaging through the land on a lonely path.

She continues to run from the rival pack that hunts her because she is a Phantom Wolf. Attracted to a scent, Sia finds her old best friend, who is now a grown woman. Having once saved Keeley, Sia takes the role of protector yet again, despite Keeley's involvement with the mysterious Alpha, Kiba, and his kin brother, Saith. An ambush separates the pack and the four of them blindly fight the new warriors that attack them: desperately needing to find out where the attacks are coming from, as Sia has vowed to protect Keeley. But at what cost?

Now being chased, Sia finds herself conflicted by the mortal and spirit world while trying to protect her kin. Sia must confront her fears, as well as the human lover who killed her many years before. It is not only survival Sia contends with, but her own façade that must be broken so that she may find peace within herself once more.

The Three Immortal Blades

Contains the entire Award Winning Collection. Karla Gray is an ordinary young woman that is taken from her mundane life into a world of blood lust as she begins to struggle with a unique ability. Karla is a Shielder; an exceptional fighter born with the rare ability to project a Shield for protection. However, Shielders are not the only kind that possesses such a talent. The Shielders battle a war that has been raging for centuries against Starkorfs, who harvest humans and Shielders alike to obtain a near immortality. Alongside the charming Lucas and selfless Paul, Karla must unravel the purpose of her curse and battle an unknown presence manipulating her thoughts; a mysterious woman who may be dormant for now, but has every intention of possessing Karla- mind, body, and soul. Within this new reality that Karla faces the search for the Three Immortal Blades begins.